MONSIEUR PAMPLEMOUSSE AND THE CARBON FOOTPRINT

Michael Bond

CHIVERS

British Library Cataloguing in Publication Data available

This Large Print edition published by BBC Audiobooks Ltd, Bath, 2010.
Published by arrangement with Allison & Busby Ltd

U.K. Hardcover ISBN 978 1 408 49243 7
U.K. Softcover ISBN 978 1 408 49244 4

Printed and bound in Great Britain by
CPI Antony Rowe, Chippenham and Eastbourne

CHAPTER ONE

Véronique put a finger to her lips before gently opening the door. 'If I were you,' she whispered, 'I would keep it low key. We're a bit edgy today . . .'

Murmuring his thanks, Monsieur Pamplemousse signalled Pommes Frites to follow on behind as they tiptoed past the Director's secretary into the Holy of Holies.

Glancing quickly round the room, he seated himself in a chair standing ready and waiting opposite Monsieur Leclercq's vast desk. Pommes Frites, meanwhile, hastened to make himself comfortable on the deep pile carpet at his feet.

Clearly, Véronique had not been exaggerating. All the signs suggested that if anything she was understating the situation.

Normally a model of sartorial elegance, the Head of France's premier gastronomic guide looked in a sorry state; his Marcel Lassance tie hung loose around his neck, the jacket of his André Bardot suit was draped higgledy-piggledy over the back of a chair, and although one sleeve of the Eglé bespoke shirt was neatly rolled back above his elbow, the other looked as though it might have been involved in a close encounter with a lawnmower . . . perhaps while adjusting the blades, although that was

1

highly improbable.

Unlike the past President of France, Monsieur Jacques Chirac, who was credited with having once operated a forklift truck in an American brewery following a spell at Harvard University, Monsieur Pamplemousse doubted if the Director had ever got his hands dirty in the whole of his life. The generally accepted opinion was that he probably laid out the ground rules at an early age; demonstrating clearly to all and sundry that even such mundane tasks as changing a typewriter ribbon were beyond his powers, making sure that letters dictated during the course of the day arrived without fail on his desk ready for signing at the appointed time that same afternoon. The licking of envelopes would have been someone else's responsibility, thus allowing his taste buds to remain unsullied by close contact with gum mucilage.

Discretion being the better part of valour, it was probably far better to hold his fire until a suitable moment arose. After what seemed like an eternity, and aware of a certain restiveness at his feet, he could stand it no longer.

'You sent for us, Monsieur?' he ventured.

'Yes, yes, Pamplemousse,' said the Director distantly. 'But it was you I wished to have words with first of all.'

Pausing as he riffled through the pile of papers, he glanced pointedly at the figure on

2

the floor.

'Would you prefer it if Pommes Frites waited outside?' asked Monsieur Pamplemousse.

'No, no,' said Monsieur Leclercq gruffly. 'It's just that . . . well, to put it bluntly, Aristide, you are rather earlier than I expected and I have important matters to discuss. My mind is in turmoil and it is hard to concentrate when your every move is subject to scrutiny by two pairs of eyes rather than one.'

Ever sensitive to the prevailing atmosphere, and sufficiently conversant with the use of certain key words, Pommes Frites settled down again and, with his tail at half-mast, pretended to busy himself with his ablutions, although clearly his heart wasn't in it.

'Your message sounded urgent,' said Monsieur Pamplemousse. 'That being the case, we came as quickly as we could. It just so happened the traffic lights were green all the way. Such a thing has never happened before.'

'Aaah!' His words fell on deaf ears as an exclamation from the Director indicated he had at long last found what he had been looking for.

He waved aloft a crumpled form between thumb and forefinger. 'As you will doubtless remember, Pamplemousse, I recently issued a questionnaire to all members of staff.

'I had in mind ascertaining their views on various matters of importance. It was all part of an exercise in reappraising our current

3

position in this difficult world of ours. Running an operation the size of *Le Guide* is a costly exercise, and from time to time, in common with most large companies, we have to take stock of the most expensive item of all: namely, manpower. It was our accountants who first posed the question. Are we, they asked, always getting value for money from those who work in the field?'

Monsieur Pamplemousse essayed a non-committal response, wondering what could possibly be coming next and fearing the worst.

'Cast your mind back,' continued the Director, 'and you may also recall the very first question on the list.'

'As a member of France's premier food guide, what are the three things uppermost in your mind at all times?' said Monsieur Pamplemousse.

In spite of himself, the Director looked impressed. 'That is correct, Pamplemousse. Which makes your answer, "Sex, money, and still more sex," singularly disappointing, even by present day standards.'

Monsieur Pamplemousse gave a start. 'But . . .' half rising from his chair, he held out a free hand, 'may I see that form, Monsieur?'

The Director smoothed the piece of paper carefully on a blotting pad before handing it over. 'I must confess, I was so incensed by your answer I screwed it into a ball and threw it into the waste bin. Unfortunately, my hand was

4

trembling so I missed the target and it landed in a vase of flowers. The cleaning lady retrieved it for me later that day and left it on my desk to dry.'

'Where would we be without the cleaning ladies of this world?' mused Monsieur Pamplemousse, sinking back into his chair. 'Hortense is a treasure and no mistake.'

'Is that her name?' said Monsieur Leclercq. 'I had no idea.'

'Speaking from experience,' continued Monsieur Pamplemousse, savouring a minor victory, 'I venture to suggest the answer which so upset you probably reflects the view of the vast majority of the French population, the younger ones in particular. It is a characteristic of our nation that its citizens take the business of living and all its many and varied ramifications seriously.'

Holding the paper up to the light, he studied it carefully. 'Having said that, I must inform Monsieur that this is not my handwriting . . .'

'Not your handwriting, Pamplemousse?' boomed the Director. 'If it is not your handwriting, then how did it come to grace a form which has your name at the top?'

'That,' said Monsieur Pamplemousse grimly, 'is a question I shall address as soon as possible.'

A joke was a joke, but there were limits. He strongly suspected Glandier. The schoolboy in him was never far away. Blessed with a distorted sense of humour, his colleague's prowess as a performer of conjuring tricks at staff parties all too often extended itself to other forms of trickery when he was at a loose end.

'I accept what you say, Aristide,' said Monsieur Leclercq, 'albeit with a certain amount of reluctance.'

'It is an area where there are those who say I am accident prone,' admitted Monsieur Pamplemousse.

'Prone you may be while it is happening, Pamplemousse,' said Monsieur Leclercq sternly, 'but more often than not I fear it is no accident.

'That is why I fell victim to a jest that was in very poor taste. I am relieved to hear my faith in you is not entirely misplaced. The correct answer, as I am sure you will agree, is first and foremost the well-being of *Le Guide*, closely followed by carbon footprints and global warming.'

Monsieur Pamplemousse remained silent. He wondered how many of his colleagues lived up to such high ideals. As ever, the Director was out of touch with reality. Speaking personally, pleased though he was to know Monsieur Leclercq's faith in him had been restored, he could barely lay claim to always observing the first item on the list, let alone the other two.

'The phrase "carbon footprint" does seem to

be on everybody's lips these days,' he said, non-committally. 'Next year it will doubtless be something else. These things tend to have a limited shelf life. The journals seize on whatever is currently in vogue and work it to death.'

'All creatures, no matter what their size, leave a carbon footprint,' said Monsieur Leclercq reprovingly. 'Whether by accident or design, it is a God-given fact of life and it is something that will not change. One must never forget that, Aristide.

'Centipedes, ants, earwigs, even the humble escargot . . . they all have their place in the scheme of things. They arrive on this earth hard-wired from the word go.'

Picking up on the phrase 'hard-wired', Monsieur Pamplemousse's heart sank. The words had a definite transatlantic ring to them. It suggested Monsieur Leclercq had just returned from one of his periodic trips to the United States. They often boded ill.

'I grant you,' continued the Director, 'that given its overall dimensions in terms of height, length and width, an escargot's carbon footprint alongside that of, say, an elephant, is hard to evaluate.'

Pausing to sweep the pile of papers to one side, he leant back in his chair.

'However, it brings me to another matter currently exercising my mind, and which happens to be one of the reasons why I

7

summoned you here today.'

Monsieur Pamplemousse listened with only half an ear. *Le Guide*'s logo—two escargots rampant—was a constantly recurring concern of the Director and there was little more he could contribute to the subject. Leaving aside the use of the words 'hard-wired', the phrase '*one* of the reasons' was also unsettling. It sounded as though there might be a whole catalogue of them.

Monsieur Leclercq picked up a silver paperweight cast in the shape of the subject under discussion.

'Apart from the fact that, strictly speaking, our logo is no longer politically correct, in many respects it no longer reflects the kind of dynamic image we need to project in this day and age, when the emphasis everywhere is on speed. This is particularly true when it comes to our readers on the other side of the Atlantic Ocean. In my experience, they are mostly blind to the humble *helix pomotia*'s virtues as a delicacy. Following considerable research, I have yet to see escargots feature on any American menu.

'However, that is by the by. The inescapable truth is that sales of *Le Guide* in the United States of America have plummeted over the past year.'

To prove his point he held up a graph showing a long red line which not only dipped alarmingly as it neared the right-hand edge of the paper, but disappeared entirely before reaching it.

'We are not alone, of course. Michelin have had their problems too, although they are fighting back. As you know, their logo has recently been updated. Monsieur Bibendum has shed a roll of fat and is looking all the better for it. He is now a leaner, fitter image of his former roly-poly self; and in so doing he has become an example to us all.'

'That kind of thing can backfire,' said Monsieur Pamplemousse. 'My understanding is that many people in America set great store by rolls of fat. They call them "love handles".'

'Is that so, Pamplemousse?' said the Director distastefully. 'I am happy to take your word for it.

'Be that as it may, our chief rival in the United States is a publication called *Zagat*, a guide that relies for its information on reports sent in by readers, who offer up their experiences when dining out. Given that more often than not they dwell on the size and quantity of fried potatoes, it is little wonder many of them have a weight problem.'

Monsieur Pamplemousse felt his pulse begin to quicken. Could it be that the Director was dangling a promotional carrot before his eyes? Head of the long-mooted American office, perhaps?

There would be snags, of course, but it was an exciting prospect. Pommes Frites would probably need to have a chip listing all his relevant details implanted somewhere or other on his person before being allowed into the country . . . that could be why the Director was choosing his words with care. He would know, of course, that Monsieur Pamplemousse would never contemplate going to America without him. It must also be the reason why he had been invited along to the meeting.

That apart, he wasn't at all sure how his wife would take the news. Knowing Doucette, she would be worried about what to wear for a start.

He tried dipping his toes into the water. 'For some while now Pommes Frites and I have been metaphorically girding our respective loins ready for our next assignment . . .' he began, hastily cutting short what he had been about to say as he realised the Director was still dwelling on the subject of snails.

'I fear the worst, Aristide,' said Monsieur Leclercq. 'Storm clouds are already gathering on the horizon for the gastropods of this world.'

'They come ready equipped to withstand any amount of sudden downpours,' said Monsieur Pamplemousse.

'It is not that aspect of it which bothers me,' said the Director. 'It is our image.'

'In that case,' suggested Monsieur Pamplemousse, 'could we not generate a little more publicity? A spectacular win in the field

10

of international sport, perhaps? In *Grande-Bretagne* they hold an annual World Championship Race for snails. Last year's winner completed the 33cm course in 2 minutes 49 seconds and won a tankard full of lettuce leaves.'

'Hardly headline news, Pamplemousse,' said Monsieur Leclercq dubiously. 'In the field of sport it hardly ranks alongside the furore that accompanied the first 4-minute mile.

'Besides, a lot can happen to an escargot even in that short distance. A passing blackbird could swoop down and make off with it long before it crossed the finishing line, and then where would we be?

'All that apart, my understanding is that supplies are dwindling. Many now come from as far away as Bulgaria. The climate changes we have been experiencing of late do nothing to help matters. The winters last much longer and they are growing colder. Escargots take anything up to six hours to copulate and even then it is very much a hit and miss affair.'

'I suppose,' mused Monsieur Pamplemousse, 'for an escargot, life is a matter of swings and roundabouts. Could we not use science to help them along? A little Viagra sprinkled on their lettuce leaves, perhaps?'

'I think not.' The Director gave a shudder. 'Who knows what might be unleashed?'

'In that case, perhaps it is time we changed our logo?'

'Change our logo?' boomed the Director. 'That is out of the question. Our Founder set great store by it. He would turn in his grave.'

Monsieur Pamplemousse took the opportunity to glance at the portrait of *Le Guide*'s Founder on the wall above the drinks cupboard to his left. Depending on the light, Monsieur Hippolyte Duval had an uncanny way of reflecting the prevailing atmosphere, but for once it offered no clues. Bathed in sunshine streaming through the vast picture window behind the Director, he looked extremely non-committal, almost as though he had washed his hands of whatever it was that was exercising Monsieur Leclercq's mind.

A passing cloud momentarily threw a shadow across the Founder's face, causing Monsieur Pamplemousse to decide 'fed up to the back teeth' might be a better description. Or, could it be that he was issuing some kind of a warning? It was hard to say. All the same, he couldn't help but agree with the Director. They must tread carefully.

'At all costs we must avoid doing anything untoward,' he said out loud. 'It would be a breach of faith.'

'*Exactement*,' said the Director, completely oblivious to the other's thoughts. 'However, we do have a fundamental problem in that escargots are, by their very nature, slow-moving creatures. From birth they are hardly equipped to exceed the speed limit wherever

12

they happen to be going. They lack the get up and go spirit one associates with our friends on the other side of the Atlantic. Overtaking another escargot is not something that would ever occur to them. Pile-ups would be rife.'

'Could you not add wheels to the ones on our logo?' said Monsieur Pamplemousse. 'Or perhaps even mount them on a motorised scooter? The suggestion of exhaust fumes and the wearing of goggles along with bending over the handlebars would create an illusion of speed. Either that, or you could have them make use of one of those exercise machines with an endless belt. I believe they are very popular in American homes, and such an image could help no end with their carbon footprints.'

'This is no joking matter, Pamplemousse,' said Monsieur Leclercq severely. 'However, I do congratulate you for putting your finger on exactly the right spot as always. Mention of exercise machines happens to be particularly apposite at this juncture. I have already been toying with the idea of converting the bar area in the canteen into a gymnasium.'

Monsieur Pamplemousse sank back in his chair. It was all much worse than he had pictured. Such an idea would go down like a lead balloon. Strike action would be the order of the day once word got around.

'As you are well aware, Pamplemousse,' continued the Director, 'this is not the first time I have had to draw your attention to the fact that your own carbon footprint leaves much to be desired. As for Pommes Frites . . . his paws appear to have reached danger level. I hate to think how many units of wine he consumes on his travels.'

Monsieur Pamplemousse stared at the Director. How could he?

'With respect, Monsieur,' he said, taking up the cudgels on behalf of his friend and mentor, and with dreams of a temporary posting to America fading fast, 'dogs do not recognise units. I doubt if Pommes Frites knows the meaning of the word. As for the size of his paws; may I remind you that they are attached to his legs and he has four of those in all. That being so, and notwithstanding the size of the whole, I venture to suggest his carbon footprint must compare favourably with the average escargot. It is like the old Citroën Light Fifteen. That, too, had a wheel at each corner and was much prized by the Paris Police for its weight distribution—'

'Legs . . . paws . . .' broke in Monsieur Leclercq, 'they are both problem areas and neither of you are alone in that respect.

'It is another area that is of concern to the accountants. The group insurance rate for our inspectors is the highest for the whole organisation. Only the other day, Madame Grante reminded me of the fact that according to the Association of Insurance Actuaries, the

14

life expectancy of an average food inspector is less than that of a garbage collector in Outer Mongolia . . . her memo made depressing reading.'

'Most of Madame Grante's memos make depressing reading,' said Monsieur Pamplemousse. 'Besides, it is all very well for her. She hardly eats more than a mouse on a diet; her own carbon footprint doesn't bear thinking about. It must be the size of a flea's.

'As for those of us out on the road, sampling dishes across the length and breadth of France, I grant you weight *is* an occupational hazard. Two meals a day, week in and week out, may sound like a dream occupation to most people, but it can be quite the reverse. I count myself fortunate in having Pommes Frites always at my side, in a state of constant readiness to help out when required.

'Furthermore, if I may say so, the Association of Insurance Actuaries fails to take account of the fact that the "Silent Forks" column of our staff magazine, commemorating those who have passed away, has, over the years, been entirely made up of staff who were desk-bound. Since I joined the company no inspector has yet shed his mortal coil during the course of duty.'

It was a long and spirited speech, and even Pommes Frites looked up admiringly at his master when he finally came to an end.

'*Yet* is the key word, Aristide,' said Monsieur

Leclercq mildly.

'Perhaps,' said Monsieur Pamplemousse, 'in order to ensure I am not the first, I should, for the second time in my life, take early retirement.'

Clearly, he had struck a nerve. The Director went pale at the thought.

'You mustn't even consider it, Aristide,' he said. 'Certainly not at this present juncture. I would hate anything to happen to you, and I am only speaking for your own good. Which is why . . .' he began playing nervously with the logo, 'which is the main reason why I have called you in at this early hour.'

The fact that from time to time Monsieur Leclercq had been using his given name hadn't escaped Monsieur Pamplemousse's notice. It was an old ploy. Get rid of various irksome matters first, undermine the opposition's confidence with threats of possible reprisals over minor matters, leaving them wondering what would happen next. Then, and only then, soften your approach. The Director was a dab hand at it. Not for nothing was he a product of a French *grande école.*

If past form was anything to go by, the true reason for their being summoned was about to be revealed.

'What is the best thing that ever happened to you, Aristide?' asked Monsieur Leclercq, settling back in his chair once again.

Momentarily thrown, and sensing he might

16

unwittingly be trapped into doing something he didn't want to do, Monsieur Pamplemousse gave careful consideration to his response.

'Leaving aside the obvious things, like meeting my dear wife, I would say the moment when I retired from the *Sûreté* and they gave me Pommes Frites as a leaving present.'

'And the worst?'

'The day in the South of France when he disappeared into the Nice sewerage system and I thought he was lost for ever. If you remember, Monsieur, Doucette and I were taking a holiday in Juan-les-Pins. We had been planning to spend it in Le Touquet, but you very kindly suggested the change in return for picking up a painting in Nice on behalf of Madame Leclercq.

'It got off to a bad start when we had to witness a performance of *West Side Story*, given by the mixed infants at a nearby Russian School. Then, you may recall, that very same night a dismembered body was washed up outside our hotel, and from then on it was downhill all the way.'

Monsieur Leclercq gave a shudder. 'Please don't remind me, Pamplemousse,' he said. 'There are some things I would much sooner forget.'

'When Pommes Frites finally emerged,' persisted Monsieur Pamplemousse, 'he wasn't exactly smelling of roses.'

'May I ask what is the second thing which

springs to mind, Aristide?' asked Monsieur Leclercq casually.

Sensing the other's disappointment and putting two and two together, Monsieur Pamplemousse essayed a stab in the dark. 'Undoubtedly the day when, quite by chance, we bumped into each other in the street,' he said. 'That, too, came about through Pommes Frites. We were taking a walk together.'

Monsieur Leclercq looked relieved. 'I don't know what I would have done without you all these years, Aristide,' he said simply. 'It was a happy chance that led us to meet as we did.'

'One turns a corner,' said Monsieur Pamplemousse, 'and one's whole life changes. I certainly have no cause for regret.'

'I have a big favour to ask of you, Aristide.'

'Monsieur has only to ask,' said Monsieur Pamplemousse, privately wishing the Director would get on with whatever it was he had in mind.

'Glancing through your P27,' said Monsieur Leclercq, 'I see that, apart from the many accomplishments you list, particularly those acquired during your time in the police force, weapon training and so on, you are clearly not without literary aspirations.'

'A great deal of my time in the Paris *Sûreté* was spent writing reports,' said Monsieur Pamplemousse. 'In some respects it is a very bureaucratic organisation. One always endeavoured to make them as clear and succinct as possible; marshalling the facts to prove the point in such a way as to leave no room for doubt. Defending lawyers are past masters in the art of ferreting out any loophole in the law.'

'Have you ever thought of taking your writing more seriously?'

Monsieur Pamplemousse shook his head. 'Since joining *Le Guide* all I have done is contribute a few articles to *L'Escargot*.'

'The staff magazine would have been all the poorer without them,' said the Director. 'I particularly enjoyed your last piece, "Whither *le coq au vin*".'

Monsieur Pamplemousse was beginning to wonder where the conversation was leading. It felt as though they were getting nowhere very fast.

'Apart from one or two outlying districts in Burgundy,' he said, 'the dish is becoming more and more of a rarity. Its preparation is time consuming and, as you wisely remarked earlier, the emphasis everywhere these days is on speed. As for my taking up writing, that also requires time. And thinking time is becoming a rare luxury these days.'

'That being the case, Aristide,' said Monsieur Leclercq, 'how would you feel if I were to grant you a few weeks unofficial leave? Over and above your normal quota, of course,' he added hastily. 'Both you and Pommes Frites have been very busy on extra curricular activities of late. You could do with some quality time at home.'

'I must admit,' said Monsieur Pamplemousse, 'that when I first joined *Le Guide* I pictured leading a more tranquil life. In many respects, as Doucette reminded me only the other day, it has been quite the reverse.

'There was that unfortunate affair involving your wife's Uncle Caputo. His connections with the Mafia must be a constant source of worry to you.

'Prior to that there was the case of the poisoned chocolates . . . If you remember, Pommes Frites accidentally overdosed on some aphrodisiac tablets and ran amok among the canine guests in the Pommes d'Or hotel. It's a wonder people still take their pets with them when they stay there.

'Then, more recently, there was your unfortunate encounter with the young lady who was masquerading as a nun on the flight back from America. The one who invited you to join the Mile High Club . . .'

'Please, Pamplemousse, I do not wish to be reminded of these things.' Monsieur Leclercq held up his hand. 'You have yet to answer my question.'

Monsieur Pamplemousse chose his words with care. 'The suggestion is not without its attractions, Monsieur. On the other hand, I find it hard to picture being idle for that length of time . . .'

'Oh, you won't be idle, Aristide,' broke in the Director. 'Not at this particular juncture. You can rest assured on that score.'

There it was again! Monsieur Pamplemousse's eyes narrowed. 'When you use the word "juncture", Monsieur,' he said, 'what exactly do you mean?'

'Really, Aristide . . .' Monsieur Leclercq brushed aside the question impatiently, much as he might dispose of an errant fly about to make a forced landing in his glass of d'Yquem. 'The word "juncture" simply underlines the fact that at this point in time we have reached a *moment critique* in our fortunes. A window of opportunity has presented itself, which, if all goes well, will provide us with a golden opportunity to hit a home run.'

Monsieur Pamplemousse winced. Anyone less likely than the Director to hit a home run in the accepted sense of the word would be hard to imagine.

'Am I to take it, Monsieur, that you have a solution in mind, and that I can help in some way?'

'That,' said Monsieur Leclercq, 'sums the whole thing up in the proverbial nutshell.

'I am not normally superstitious, Aristide,' he continued, 'but when I woke this morning and found not one but *two* blackbirds perched on my bedroom window sill, I feared the worst. I mistrust one blackbird, but two . . .

'Then, when my wife explained to me that not only was it a good omen, but a singularly rare one at that, I felt a sudden surge of excitement. It was a case of cause and effect. Chantal's enthusiasm was contagious. On my way into the office this morning the way ahead and the solution to our problems in America became clear.'

Monsieur Pamplemousse exchanged glances with Pommes Frites as the Director crossed to the door, made sure it was properly shut, then returned to his desk and, having phoned Véronique to ensure they were not disturbed, sat back in his chair and beamed at them.

The preliminaries off his chest so to speak, he was starting to look positively rejuvenated, almost as though a great weight had been lifted from his mind.

'I knew I could rely on you, Aristide,' he said. 'In fact . . .' breaking off, he rose to his feet again and headed for the drinks cabinet.

'I think it calls for a celebration. Some of your favourite Gosset champagne, perhaps? Or shall I open a bottle of the Roullet *très hors age* cognac?' His hand hovered over the glasses. 'The choice is yours. Which is it to be?'

Monsieur Pamplemousse hesitated. He was unaware of having even remotely agreed to anything. 'I hope you won't think I am being difficult,' he said, 'but without knowing exactly what we are celebrating it is hard to reach a decision.'

He should have known better.

For a brief moment Monsieur Leclercq looked suitably chastened. 'You are absolutely right, Aristide,' he exclaimed. 'I am so excited by the turn of events I am getting ahead of myself.'

He struck one of his Napoleonic poses; a pose honed to perfection over the years by taking in the view from his window of the Emperor's last resting place beneath the golden dome of the nearby Hôtel des Invalides.

'Pamplemousse,' he said grandly, 'I have a plan of campaign! It is my wish to run it up the flagpole and see if, in your view, it flies.

'If your answer is in the affirmative, then it is really a question of pulling all the right levers, and for that we shall need what is known as a road map.'

Monsieur Pamplemousse gloomily opted for a glass of champagne. It was a good buck-you-up at any time of the day or night, and he suddenly felt in need of one.

*   *   *

'Monsieur Leclercq has a plan?' repeated Doucette over dinner. 'I don't like the sound of that.'

'It is what he calls a "road map", Couscous,' said Monsieur Pamplemousse. 'I must say I

23

was a bit sceptical myself at first.'

'How many weeks will it take you?'

'That all depends on how many dead ends I come across,' said Monsieur Pamplemousse vaguely. He toyed with the remains of his dessert. 'It needs to be in place before the start of the racing season in Deauville.'

'It would never do to miss that,' said Doucette dryly.

'It is all mixed up with the annual staff party at his summer residence,' said Monsieur Pamplemousse. 'As always, wives are invited too, only this year, if all goes well, there will be an extra guest; a very important one.'

'July? That's over two months away.'

'Just think,' said Monsieur Pamplemousse. 'All that time at home.' He spooned the remains of the dessert onto his plate. 'Once again, Couscous, tell me the recipe for this delicious concoction. What is it called? *Crème bachique?*'

'Bacchus Delight,' said Doucette, 'is a baked custard made with half a litre or so of Sauternes, six egg yolks, four ounces of sugar and a touch of cinnamon.'

'But made with love,' said Monsieur Pamplemousse. 'That is the most important ingredient, Couscous.'

He gave a sigh of satisfaction. 'It is good to be home. White asparagus from the Landes with sauce mousseline—one of my favourites; sole, pan-fried in butter, seasoned with parsley

24

and lemon and served with tiny new potatoes; and now Bacchus Delight . . . what more could any man wish for? Simple dishes, all of them, but as I have so often said in the past, anyone can follow a recipe. It takes love and understanding to bring a meal to full fruition. It is what is known as "the passion".'

'If you and Pommes Frites are planning to be around for two whole months, don't expect to eat like this every day of the week,' said Doucette, as she bustled around clearing the table. 'Besides, there are all sorts of things that need attending to. The window boxes could do with a thorough going over for a start. I will make a list . . .'

'First things first,' said Monsieur Pamplemousse hurriedly. 'It is a matter of priorities.'

'In that case,' said Doucette, 'I suggest you start by telling me exactly what Monsieur Leclercq has in mind.'

'Ah!' Monsieur Pamplemousse looked at his watch. 'Now that, Couscous, is going to take time. Time, and a measure of understanding. Perhaps, as an aid to digesting it all, before I begin we should open another bottle of Meursault? It involves my writing a play.'

Pommes Frites looked from one to the other before settling down in a corner of the room. A good deal of the conversation that day had gone over his head, but he knew the signs. Weighing up the pros and cons and coming down heavily on the side of the cons, it seemed to him his master might well be in need of support before the night was out.

CHAPTER TWO

The project began slowly at first. The first three days were a total blank. On day four, fed up with staring fruitlessly into space and in need of fresh air, Monsieur Pamplemousse sought inspiration from the statue of Marcel Aymé, the top half of which protruded from the brickwork outside their apartment block in Montmartre.

But the late author of *The Man Who Walked Through Walls*—the story of a humble bank clerk whose exploits had the police at their wits' end, remained singularly unmoved, as well he might. Incarcerated for posterity by his own creation, he clearly had enough problems of his own.

There were times when Monsieur Pamplemousse wished he'd never agreed to take on the task; days which felt as though they would never end, and when he did finally put his laptop to bed, he found himself lying awake in a cold sweat, convinced he would never make the deadline.

He knew he wasn't easy to live with. Conversation at the table was minimal and even Pommes Frites took to giving him funny looks when they were out for a walk. In short, communication with those around him was at a low ebb.

Then one morning, aided and abetted by his subconscious, the muse struck and he woke with the germ of an idea in the back of his mind. Hadn't it often been like that in the old days when he was a police officer? Just when things were at their blackest, a glimmer of light appeared at the end of the tunnel.

Almost imperceptibly, things began to pick up. At first he was hardly aware of it, but gradually one day merged with another, the days became weeks, and the weeks turned first of all into a month, then two.

Eventually, one day in early July, he was able to sit back and relax.

'*Fini!*' he announced. 'Mission accomplished!'

It had been a close call and no mistake. Pommes Frites, without knowing quite why, wagged his tail. Doucette fetched a bottle of champagne.

'Thank goodness for that!' she exclaimed. 'I didn't think you had it in you. I really didn't.'

'I *don't* any more, Couscous,' said Monsieur Pamplemousse. 'I have let it all out.'

It was true. He felt drained.

'At least we have had you at home for a while,' said Doucette. 'But really, Aristide, I don't know what the Director would do without you.'

'I don't know what *we* would do without Monsieur Leclercq,' countered Monsieur Pamplemousse. 'I must call him straight away and give him the good news. There is still a lot to be done and not much time left.'

And now, two weeks later, here he was, in the grounds of the Leclercqs' summer residence in Normandy, about to face his biggest test of all.

For a moment his misgivings returned. Had he overstretched—not just himself, but the others too, most of all Monsieur Leclercq, who would be bearing the brunt?

Par exemple, would there be problems with the trapdoors? Given the lack of rehearsal time they could prove hazardous. Time would tell. In a couple of hours or so, for better or worse, it would all be over.

In an effort to take his mind off a feeling of impending doom in the pit of his stomach, he gazed at the scene spread out in front of him.

Nestling in a wooded pocket of the Pays d'Auge area midway between Deauville and Pont l'Evêque, the Leclercqs' picturesque black and white half-timbered house was reached by a long driveway that wound its way down the hillside. Apart from the occasional drone of a passing light aircraft towing a banner advertising the forthcoming start of the racing season in Deauville, it could have been in another world; a million kilometres away from civilisation.

In the months ahead, the same aircraft would doubtless pass overhead highlighting other seasonal attractions as they came and went; golf matches, international bridge tournaments, jazz concerts, and later in the year, the annual film festival. But for the time being peace reigned; the sun was shining, the birds were singing, and as a string quartet struck up a lively tune, a feeling of enchantment set in.

The Director's party was an annual event, a champagne occasion, and one Monsieur Pamplemousse had experienced many times before, but even so, the sheer perfection of the surroundings was hard to take in at a glance. Somehow it always felt as though he had taken a step back in time to a more leisurely, more mannered age, with everyone suitably dressed for the occasion.

Reaching into a hip pocket, he withdrew his Leica C-Lux2, and was about to record the scene for posterity when he heard the sound of squealing tyres somewhere in the distance.

Hastily pressing the button, Monsieur Pamplemousse glanced up and was just in time to see a car sweep through the wrought-iron entrance gates. Clearly the driver was in a hurry.

Weaving its way past weeping willows and beech trees, and around the freshly tonsured lawns before skirting a Norman dovecote, it followed the path of a stream that eventually cascaded into a pond the size of a small lake. Even the ducks had a superior look on their faces as they floated gently to and fro with never a feather out of place.

As the car finally disappeared from view behind a group of red rose bushes near the house—*Danse du Feu,* if he remembered correctly, and in full bloom for the occasion; the head gardener's life would not have been worth living had they not been—Monsieur Pamplemousse came back down to earth.

It was hard not to feel envious of it all, yet at the same time easy to understand why Monsieur and Madame Leclercq always referred to the estate rather dismissively as their 'summer hideaway'. Doucette had put her finger on it, as usual. During the long winter months, deprived of guests, it would be a very different kettle of fish. The Leclercqs' only neighbours would be the inhabitants of the nearest village, and most of those probably kept themselves strictly to themselves behind shuttered windows.

Popular with tourists during the holiday season, seeking out the fourteenth-century church with its stained-glass windows and collection of Jean Restout paintings, there wouldn't be a single stranger to be seen in the village from October onwards.

He wondered if that was why Monsieur Leclercq was said to have contributed heavily towards converting the church hall into a small theatre.

Loudier, doyen of the inspectors, had a theory that Monsieur Leclercq's sights were fixed on becoming the local mayor, but since aspirations on that score already lay nearer his main home outside Paris, that seemed unlikely. Unless, of course, as Guilot suspected, he was hedging his bets and had bigger things in mind. Over half the membership of the National Assembly was made up of those holding the twin title of mayor. Acting as a springboard for higher office, it had certainly been the chosen route for many of France's presidents, including Mitterand, Chirac and, more recently, Nicolas Sarkozy.

Monsieur Pamplemousse wouldn't put it past the Director. To be a candidate for such high office needed the approval of 500 mayors, but with almost 40,000 in the whole country it wasn't beyond the bounds of possibility to drum up sufficient support.

Once again, time would tell. For the time being, such matters must be far from Monsieur Leclercq's mind as the vast patio of his country estate echoed to the buzz of conversation, interspersed at regular intervals by bursts of laughter.

Ever the perfect host, the Director was in his element overseeing the barbecue. From where he was standing, Monsieur Pamplemousse could see his white chef's hat bobbing up and down as he made sure the needs of his guests were attended to.

He was assisted in the task by a bevy of apple-cheeked girls in traditional costume. They looked as though they might have been hand-picked from Central Casting, and in truth many of them probably had been; the Director was a stickler for detail.

If past occasions were anything to go by, the barbecue itself would be fuelled by a selection of dried wood chippings from trees on his estate; chestnut for the *entrecôte* steak, its flavour enhanced by virtue of having first been marinated in olive oil and then wrapped in a caul. Chicken and lamb, on the other hand, would be brought to the peak of perfection by heat from smouldering branches of apple, peach and juniper.

Pork would have been marinated overnight in local cider and lemon, whilst smoke-producing herbs—rosemary, sage and thyme— would add their mite to the scent that filled the air.

To cater for everyone's taste, there would be stuffed vine leaves, oysters cooked in their shells, grilled lobsters, cheese on toasted bread and quiche Lorraine; not to mention both white and black *boudin*, and a variety of other sausages galore.

As for cold collations, if tables could be said to literally groan under excess weight, the air would have been filled with strange woodland oaths.

And for those who still had any room left for dessert, there was a separate area catering for their needs.

Monsieur Pamplemousse wished he could have joined in the festivities, but he felt too keyed up. He glanced at his watch. The Director was clearly in his element and it was to be hoped he was keeping a note of the time. It would never do for him to be late.

To one side of the main party, he spotted Madame Leclercq deep in conversation with a familiarly rotund figure, that of the surprise guest of honour, Jay Corby, the renowned and much-feared American gourmet, and focal point of today's exercise.

He was drinking something dark out of a large glass.

The scourge of eating establishments everywhere, restaurateurs went pale when they saw his name on the guest list. He was said to wield as much influence in the sphere of food as Robert Parker did in the world of wine. Not exactly given to hiding his light under a bushel, his reputation arrived before him wherever he went. A bad review could mean empty scats and a slow death to anyone who happened to cross his path.

His two books, *Fishy Business* and its companion volume *Done to a Turn*, had been bestsellers—the first warning readers to avoid so-called 'sea-fresh fish' when eating out on a

Monday, since most of it had probably been delivered the week before and wouldn't be more than 'fridge-fresh' at best; the latter warning against ordering a steak 'well done', for it gave restaurants a heaven-sent opportunity to use the odd discarded cuts that would have shown up all the blemishes had they been served rare.

Both books had been on the *New York Times* bestseller list for months on end. As a result, readers of his widely syndicated columns followed his words with something verging on baited breath.

Inviting him to the annual party was a masterstroke on the Director's part. One mention in Jay Corby's column extolling the virtues of *Le Guide* would be worth its weight in gold; the equivalent of several kilometres of column space in other publications.

That in itself made it all the more important for everything to go well today.

To have captured Corby for a return visit was a feather in Monsieur Leclercq's hat, particularly as it wasn't so long ago that the food writer had attended *Le Guide's* memorable in-house event, when Pommes Frites pitted his taste buds against an array of imported hounds and, fortunately for all concerned, emerged with flying colours.

On that occasion Corby had merely been passing through Paris. He was known to be a lone wolf, rarely mixing with other food critics, but even so he had been surprisingly reticent. At one point during the contest he had sounded off in praise of American beef, as opposed to that from anywhere else in the world, but otherwise he had kept a low profile.

And now here he was again. This time flown over especially from the United States with all expenses paid.

It was a classic chicken and egg situation; if he had turned the offer down at the last minute, a couple of months' work would have gone to waste. The Director must have made Corby a sizeable offer at an early stage in the proceedings.

Had Monsieur Pamplemousse known whom the guest of honour was going to be, he might have toned his work down a little, but it was too late to worry about that now. The die was cast. He took refuge in the old adage that people seldom saw themselves as others did.

He wondered if Pommes Frites had registered the American's presence at the tasting. Preoccupied as he had been at the time, probably not; although he didn't miss much, and never forgot a face.

Come to that, he wondered where his friend and mentor had got to; he had hardly set eyes on him, or Doucette, since their arrival earlier in the day.

The question fathered the answer. At that precise moment, from his vantage point on a small hillock away from the main crowd, he caught sight of a familiar figure heading towards the house. Doubtless, Pommes Frites had also caught sight of the new arrival, and being of an enquiring disposition, was on his way to investigate the matter.

Monsieur Pamplemousse knew the signs. Pausing to leave his mark, Pommes Frites was about to take advantage of the moment to sniff the air and view the passing scene, when his ears suddenly assumed an upright position. Proceeding as though on tiptoe, he edged towards a small door let into the side of an extension to the main house and, having pushed it open with his nose, disappeared from view.

Monsieur Pamplemousse drained his glass of Chateldon water and set off in pursuit. Apart from anything else, it was high time he joined his colleagues in case they needed a last-minute pep talk.

Entering the house through the same swing door Pommes Frites had used, he made his way along a narrow corridor and through an open archway at the end. The area he found himself in must be the latest addition to the Leclercqs' property; a changing room for those making use of a swimming pool visible through sliding windows at the far end.

Obviously the pool was not in use at the moment, for the room was littered with open suitcases. Monsieur Pamplemousse came to a sudden halt as he caught sight of a shadowy

36

figure bent over one of them. Partially screened by the other luggage, whoever it was appeared to be totally unaware of Pommes Frites' presence.

For the second time that afternoon, and with a speed that would have brought a nod of approval from the acknowledged master of the *moment critique*, the late Cartier-Bresson, Monsieur Pamplemousse reached for his camera.

Short of actually turning to his master and saying 'Ssh', Pommes Frites' bearing said it all; not that words were needed. Any sound was effectively overridden by the noise from outside.

Having assured himself that his unspoken message had been received and understood, he eased himself forward, intent on doing what any other red-blooded animal would have done under the circumstances, except that, given his height, he was better equipped than most to carry out the operation successfully, for it gave him, so to speak, a head start.

Split-second timing was of the essence and, as Pommes Frites applied his moist nose to the end of his quarry, so Monsieur Pamplemousse pressed the button, and the automatic flash on his camera came into play.

The effect was instantaneous. There was a shriek, and the girl leapt to her feet as though she had been shot.

Clad only in a gold Patek Phillippe

wristwatch, she confronted Monsieur Pamplemousse.

'Pervert! What are you . . . some kind of fetishist?'

Monsieur Pamplemousse drew back. '*Excusez-moi* . . .' he began.

'*Excusez-moi* nothing! I've met your sort from here to you name it. I hope you're satisfied. You want me to upgrade my butt for your benefit? Just let me know.'

As the girl drew near, Monsieur Pamplemousse hesitated, partly stunned into silence by the stream of verbiage.

On the other hand, he couldn't deny the *derrière* Pommes Frites had set his sights on was in a class of its own. Not since his close encounter with the chorus line at the Folies— the one that had led to his taking early retirement from the Paris *Sûreté*—had he felt quite so bereft of words.

He could have dwelt at length on the outstanding quality of the girl's *balcons*. The roundness, the firmness, the provocative way each *point de sein* was pointing straight at him, or so it seemed from where he was standing. Her lips, her long black hair, her brown body . . . everything about her defied description.

As for her legs; from the beginning of the shapely ankles, they went up and up seemingly to eternity and beyond.

Following the direction of his gaze, the girl suddenly took him by surprise as she executed an impeccable high kick.

'Satisfied?' She spoke with an American accent. Wall Street English, as advertisements on the Metro would have it. 'When you've finished making an inventory I'd like to carry on getting changed. *If* you don't mind.'

'You must excuse Pommes Frites,' said Monsieur Pamplemousse hastily. 'He was simply obeying a natural curiosity.'

The girl looked down and registered the culprit for the first time. 'Yeah! Well, you know what they say. Curiosity killed the cat. What's your excuse?'

'I will make sure you have a copy of the printout,' said Monsieur Pamplemousse lamely. 'You have a wonderful carbon-neutral footprint. It is without doubt one of the most eco-friendly I have ever seen . . .'

It was the best he could do on the spur of the moment, but it stopped the girl dead in her tracks. She slowly lowered her leg.

'Nobody's ever said anything like that to me before,' she said simply.

It struck Monsieur Pamplemousse that the whites of her eyes were like snow on a mountain top. Was there no end to her virtues?

He was saved any further conjecture by an all-too-familiar booming voice. His heart sank. The Director must be taking someone on a guided tour. Worse still, it sounded as though he was heading their way.

'Quick . . .' Without waiting for an answer, he grabbed hold of the girl and propelled her towards an open door, the nearest in a row of cubicles lining the wall to his right. Pommes Frites hurried after them.

There was scarcely room for two, let alone three, and barely time to slip the bolt into place before the visitors entered the room.

'Ah, now this would appear to have been converted into some kind of changing room.' Monsieur Leclercq sounded taken aback. 'I wasn't kept informed. How very confusing . . . I will have my secretary diarise it for me. Please excuse me a moment while I reach her on the mobile . . .'

In desperation, Monsieur Pamplemousse felt for the flush. The sound of rushing water had the desired effect.

'Ah!' The Director hastily changed his tune. 'On second thoughts, I suggest we go back the way we came.'

Monsieur Pamplemousse didn't catch what was said in reply, but the person also spoke with an American accent.

'Jay,' hissed the girl into his ear as the voices died away.

'You know him?'

She stared at him. '*Know* him? That's a laugh!'

Acting on an impulse as they emerged from the cubicle, she planted a long, lingering kiss firmly on his lips. It was a stomach-churning

40

experience, as disturbing in its way as the minimalist perfume he had encountered during their time in the closet.

Letting go of Monsieur Pamplemousse, she turned and, while remaining remarkably unfazed by her state of *déshabille,* began searching through her travelling case, closely watched by Pommes Frites, who was clearly bowled over by the experience.

Having found what she had been looking for, she handed it to him.

'A small present for your master to remember me by,' she said. 'And don't forget ... If anyone asks, you haven't seen a thing.'

Wearing his 'dog of the world' expression, Pommes Frites looked suitably non-committal as he accepted the object and passed it to his master, who hastily thrust the object into a trouser pocket. It felt soft and filmy, but there was no point in arguing. Clearly the girl's mind was made up.

'We must leave you to change,' he said.

'Voir,' said the girl. 'Tell your hound all is forgiven.'

Pommes Frites wagged his tail and followed his master through into the next room and its more familiar surroundings.

Part of a complex that had started off as a simple double garage, for a while it had served as a gymnasium, after which it had grown over the years until it was almost another house. Now, for the time being, it was serving as an

41

assembly point for Monsieur Pamplemousse's colleagues.

Any worries he might have had about the encounter in the other room having been overheard vanished. Everyone was much too busy with their own problems . . . changing into their costumes, rehearsing lines.

Loudier was in the middle of telling a long story about an American, an Englishman, a German, and a Frenchman who were shipwrecked on a desert island. The Frenchman was the only one who survived to tell the tale, but he did say the sauce had been excellent.

That, too, was an annual event, that year by year grew longer with the telling, but the others laughed dutifully. Loudier was nearing retirement. They would miss him when he was gone.

'We were beginning to think you had deserted us in our hour of need,' said Truffert, buttoning up his waiter's uniform.

'I have done all I can,' said Monsieur Pamplemousse. 'The rest is up to all of you, I'm afraid. It is not my fault we were unable to have a dress rehearsal in situ. Monsieur Leclercq did his best, but the set builders were working until late last night. Apparently there were problems with the lighting system—the riggers threatened to go on strike because of the heat . . . Would you believe they cited global warming?'

'I believe anything in this day and age,' said Glandier. He was about to hold forth when he paused. 'Talking of global warming, something very eco-friendly has just floated in.'

Monsieur Pamplemousse turned and gazed at the transformation. He could hardly believe his eyes at the speed with which the girl had changed. Even Pommes Frites looked taken aback.

The rest of the room simply lapsed into stunned silence as the vision in white paused momentarily in the manner of a model about to execute a turn on the catwalk.

Before anyone had a chance to speak she blew a kiss, first of all in the direction of Monsieur Pamplemousse, then for some reason at another of his colleagues—Bernard, and finally towards Pommes Frites as he hurried across to greet her.

'Did anyone see what I saw?' asked Allard, as she went on her way.

'That was a conversation stopper and no mistake,' said Truffert. 'How about that wiggle?'

'Awesome,' said Glandier. 'Talk about a *derrière* to die for.'

'Her name's Amber,' said Bernard.

'Who told you that?' asked Allard.

'She did.'

'It's like those traffic lights they have in the UK,' said Glandier. 'Somewhere between red for danger and green for go ahead.'

'I know which I'd plump for,' said Allard dreamily. 'Did you see the way she vibrated when she walked? Revving on all eight cylinders; yet all sweetness and light.'

Remembering the outburst in the changing room, Monsieur Pamplemousse stayed silent. You never could tell with people once they were roused.

Feeling slightly put out, he stared at Bernard. 'You seem to know a lot about her.'

'That's the way it goes,' said Bernard airily. 'Some people have it, some don't. If you must know, I happened to be around when she arrived and I gave her a hand. She had just what she called "fast-tracked in" from New York, armed with a Louis Vuitton Keepall no less.

'It reminded me of that shot in *M*A*S*H* when Hot Lips arrived at their camp in a helicopter. Remember, everybody rushed forward to help her out? Except in this case she was climbing out backwards and the lazy so and so of a taxi driver couldn't even be bothered to get out and open the door for her. So I beat him to it.'

'Serves him right,' said Allard. 'It must have been a sight for sore eyes.'

'You can say that again. I can tell you something else about her. She was a dancer at the Crazy Horse until she failed the *doudounes* test.'

'Failed it?' repeated Allard. 'That's not

44

possible!'

'The distance between nipples must not exceed 27 cm,' said Bernard. 'Hers were over the limit.'

With his recent brief encounter still fresh in his mind, Monsieur Pamplemousse scotched the very idea of anything about the girl falling short of sheer perfection.

'It must have been a cold day,' said Bernard. 'It's like rubbing them with an ice cube. It can have that effect.'

'You should know,' said Allard.

'The Crazy Horse has strict rules on these things,' continued Bernard, airing his knowledge. 'No tattoos. No Botox or any other artificial enhancements. Weekly weight checks . . .'

'I thought all that might have changed since the Founder died,' said Truffert. 'Didn't the sons take over?'

'It sounds a bit like the Director,' broke in Glandier before Bernard had a chance to reply. 'Remember the time when he was on one of his health kicks and he had that tailor's dummy standing in his office . . .'

'Alphonse,' said Allard. 'It was his idea of the ideal inspector. He'd had all the details fed into a computer. Weight 76.8 kilos . . .'

'A cold bath every morning,' said Glandier. 'And no more than 2.6 mistresses during the course of a lifetime. I doubt if Alphonse would have admitted to 0.6. He was just too good to be true.'

'As I recall,' said Allard, 'I wasn't the only one who failed the test.'

'At least it didn't include the distance from the belly button to the pubis like they do at the Crazy Horse,' said Bernard, anxious to get back to the subject in hand. 'Max 13 cm; that's what makes their butt stick out—not that our friend needs any help in that area.'

'It's an ethnic thing,' agreed Truffert. 'They have a head start over the rest of us, if you forgive the comparison.'

'How do people land these jobs?' mused Glandier. 'I suppose it's a case of being in the right place at the right time with a tape measure at the ready.'

'It's tough work, but someone has to do it,' agreed Bernard. 'It's what's known as job satisfaction.'

'I expect it's like top flight concierges,' said Loudier. 'Hotels don't pay them. They pay the hotel. It works both ways; a good fixer is worth his weight in gold to the hotel, and if the guy is good at his job it's worth a premium for all the tips and back-handers that come his way.'

'When I suggested she might be good bunny material, she pooh poohed the idea,' said Bernard. 'She said she wouldn't want to risk getting myxomatosis.'

'I like a girl with a sense of humour,' broke in Glandier.

'She'll need it in her present job,' replied

Bernard. 'If you ask me, she and Jay Corby are an item. Not that you'd guess it from the look he gave her when they met up. You'd think she was some kind of pond life someone had dragged up by mistake. He went as white as a sheet.

'Anyway,' he pulled a handkerchief smeared with lipstick from a jacket pocket and held it up for all to see. 'Good works have their just reward!'

'I thought you said she was worried about catching myxomatosis?' exclaimed Glandier.

Bernard ignored the remark. Instead, he waved the handkerchief pointedly at Monsieur Pamplemousse. 'Funny thing, Aristide. It matches your shirt collar. What's your excuse?'

'I saved her from a fate worse than death,' said Monsieur Pamplemousse simply.

'You mean you let her pass,' interjected Boulet, amid renewed laughter.

Monsieur Pamplemousse looked at his watch. It seemed a suitable moment to call a halt. 'Time's up,' he said. 'Transport leaves in five minutes.'

A chorus of groans greeted his words, but it petered out as an announcement over the loudspeakers heralded the arrival of a small fleet of specially chartered coaches to take everyone to their destination.

Monsieur Leclercq had thought of everything, but for the majority of his guests the news came as a complete surprise. It was hard to say how many might have been tempted to plead an urgent appointment that afternoon had they got wind of the plan. However they were nipped in the bud by a further announcement from the Director.

Couched in ringing tones, it brooked no argument. Napoleon addressing his troops before the battle of Waterloo could hardly have been more eloquent, and if any of those present inwardly hoped the outcome would be more successful than the Emperor's had been, they wisely kept it to themselves.

Not so the members of the Fourth Estate. Having been kept under wraps, wined and dined behind the scenes, they were already seated in the last of the coaches. Cameras at the ready, they could hardly wait for the word 'go'.

As the convoy, led by the Director's black Citroën CX25 carrying the hosts and their guest of honour, passed through the gates and headed for the village, it struck Monsieur Pamplemousse that, seen from above, perhaps from the small plane still circling overhead, it must look for all the world like a rather grand funeral cortège. The pilot confirmed it a moment later as he dipped his wings in salute.

The general tone of conversation in the coach was certainly funereal. Muted *bonnes chances* were exchanged with increasing regularity as they drew near the hall, until Trigaux, *Le Guide*'s Head of the Art

Department, who came from a theatrical background, could stand it no longer and delivered a lecture on the fact that among superstitious thespians such words only had the reverse effect.

'In the world of the real theatre,' he announced, 'in order to avoid tempting Gods of ill fortune, it is considered necessary to say, "Break a leg!"'

'You're having us on,' said Glandier accusingly.

'Not at all.' Trigaux warmed to his subject. 'The true origin is lost in the mists of time, but a popular theory is that it goes back to 1865 when President Lincoln was assassinated at the Ford's theatre in Washington. The man who did it, a little known actor called John Wilkes Booth, jumped on the stage immediately after he had committed the crime and broke his leg, thus sealing his own fate.

'Ideally, it should be said to all the cast by someone other than an actor, the producer, or,' he added meaningfully, 'in this case, since the author is with us . . .'

'*Casser un jambon!*' said Monsieur Pamplemousse in response to repeated cries from the back of the coach, and immediately wished he hadn't.

What if the cast were not adequately insured? Finding out afterwards would be too late and everybody, most of all Monsieur Leclercq, would heap blame on his head.

Catching sight of the expression on his master's face, Pommes Frites, who had been doing his best to follow the conversation, but apart from picking up on the word *jambon* had failed dismally to get the gist of it, let out a howl.

Given the circumstances, it was as good a summing-up as Monsieur Pamplemousse could have wished for.

CHAPTER THREE

In the event, Monsieur Pamplemousse's worst fears failed to materialise. The reaction of everyone around him both during and after the play said it all.

When the final curtain fell the audience erupted into a standing ovation. Cries of 'Bravo!' rang out from all sides as he found himself being led onto the stage by his colleagues.

He felt embarrassed, for it had been very much a team effort.

All the same, from a personal point of view, he couldn't have been more delighted. Seeing his hard work come to life on stage exceeded his wildest dreams and he couldn't wait to hear Doucette's reaction.

Granted, most of the audience were well and truly fortified by the food and wine laid on by Monsieur and Madame Leclercq, and as a result they were in an expansive mood. Even so, the almost continuous laughter, not just by friends and relations of those taking part—which would have been understandable—but by the hard-bitten seen-it-all-before press corps, and the normally taciturn local inhabitants invited to fill the remaining seats, had been music to his ears.

Saint François de Sales had not deserted him after all. The patron saint of writers must simply have been keeping a low profile, temporarily tied up with his other charges; journalists and deaf mutes.

The source of his inspiration went back to an occasion many years before, when he had been to see the film version of Kaufman and Hart's play *The Man Who Came to Dinner.*

Starring Monty Woolley as the irascible Sheridan Whiteside—man-about-town, theatre critic, wit—it told the story of how the Great Man, having slipped and broken his hip on the doorstep of a luckless family in Vermont, was forced to take up temporary residence as an uninvited guest, wreaking havoc on their simple lives in consequence.

That, too, had been a hilarious evening. A classic of its time, it had remained indelibly etched in Monsieur Pamplemousse's mind.

For a brief while, during the worst moments of his 'writer's block', he had even wondered in desperation whether the stage rights were still available, and if they were, would it be beyond the scope of his colleagues' talents to resurrect it?

The very worst scenario would have been to come up with something so banal Corby would have taken the next plane back to America, vowing never to return. Any possibility of his reviewing *Le Guide* in a favourable light would have left the country with him.

Then, one morning, returning home from a walk with Pommes Frites, Monsieur Pamplemousse happened to take another look at Marcel Aymé's statue and the seeds of an idea entered his mind.

Supposing . . . just supposing . . . instead of having a character like Sheridan Whiteside— said to have been based on the acid-tongued theatre critic Alexander Woollcott—what if the play was an entirely original concept about a young couple who buy a derelict property in order to open a restaurant, only to find it was haunted by the ghost of a long-departed despot of a food critic?

In reality, the 'ghost' could be a down-and-out squatter with a gift of the gab who was determined to do everything in his power to rid the property of its new occupants, and by making use of a series of hidden trapdoors, was seemingly able to disappear and reappear at will—which must, of course, have been the secret behind Marcel Aymé's character in *The Man Who Walked Through Walls*.

Once the idea had taken root, the play almost began to write itself. Restaurants were in effect much like stage productions, with the cast assembling prior to opening time, ready to receive their last-minute notes on the dishes of the day before taking up their allotted positions.

The joy of it was that, steeped as they were in what went on behind the scenes, there was no need for any of his colleagues to have prior acting experience; they simply played themselves.

It was the equivalent of having a ready-made supply of staff and customers at his disposal, a cast, moreover, blessed with the built-in advantage of their arriving ready-armed with a plentiful supply of ancient 'Waiter, there's a fly in my soup' jokes. Honed to perfection by constant repetition over the years and retold with relish to a captive audience, they had taken full advantage of the situation and milked it for all it was worth.

If there was a certain amount of ad-libbing it was only to be expected and only added to the fun.

Véronique, looking stunning in an outfit specially hired for the occasion, was perfect in the part of the young wife.

Boulet, *Le Guide*'s most recent recruit, who made no bones about fancying her, had jumped at the chance of playing the husband, revelling in those moments when she was at her wits' end and in need of solace. The fact that, according to Glandier, the Director's ever-resourceful secretary had taken the precautionary measure of overdosing heavily on garlic beforehand proved no deterrent.

And if Boulet's ministrations gave rise to the very few *longeurs* there were in the play, who could blame him? Besides, they came as a welcome relief to the audience after all the laughter.

Madame Grante was also a classic example of typecasting. Dressed in black bombazine, she was tailor-made for the role of an elderly dyspeptic cashier. Seated at a high desk near the entrance to the dining room, there were times when her grumpy asides, as she dipped into her vast store of real-life grievances, threatened to bring the house down.

Trigaux, normally the most reticent of people, had surprised everyone with his state of the art electronic sound effects; howling wind, creaking stairs, the eerie cries of a banshee . . .

But it was the casting of the Director in the role of the itinerant vagrant that really paid off, exceeding even Monsieur Pamplemousse's expectations.

Had the play been put on in a normal theatre instead of a local village hall, he felt sure it would have run and run. He could picture the inscription in lights above the entrance: 'HENRI LECLERCQ—STARRING IN . . .'

Or perhaps, in the tradition of so many famous French actors over the years—Raimu, Charpin, Fernandel, to name but a few— simply 'LECLERCQ'. Undoubtedly, *Le Guide*'s director would receive even more of a standing ovation than Monsieur Pamplemousse had been granted, when he did eventually put in an appearance—and deservedly so. A frustrated thespian at heart, he had positively revelled in his part.

Lines that had seemed innocuous enough on paper became like barbed arrows when they emerged from his lips, heading straight for the centre of the target every time. Not for him any suggestion of miming. Everything had to be played for real, each morsel of food set before him was consumed with relish.

Had the ingredients been stage props, he could have been palming them, whereas in reality everything was fresh from the barbecue. Where he managed to put it all was hard to picture. It was a bravura performance, and he had seemed to grow in stature with each new appearance on stage.

As the cast took their 'final' bows in front of the curtain for what seemed like the umpteenth time—Monsieur Pamplemousse had lost count of the number—he contrived to search the wings for the star of the show.

He could, of course, be back in his dressing room removing his make-up, but that was highly unlikely. It would be totally out of character for Monsieur Leclercq to forego the plaudits of the crowd. Appearing in full make-up would be an undoubted plus.

Having drawn a blank on both sides of the proscenium arch, Monsieur Pamplemousse broke away from the others as gracefully as he could and hurried backstage. Something was clearly amiss.

Pommes Frites hesitated for a moment or two before following on behind.

Given the choice he would sooner have stayed with the others, but he staunchly resisted the temptation. In truth, although he'd only been entrusted with a walk-on part, he had caught the acting bug.

He had certainly done his level best to make the most of it, pausing to leave his mark on a potted bay tree by the entrance to the restaurant whenever he had the chance. As with the simplest of catchphrases, repetition brought its own reward, and the applause that greeted his first appearance grew in volume with each successive visit. In the end it became addictive, and when his normally ample reserves ran out he turned his back on the audience and resorted to miming. It was canine acting of the highest order.

Hearing a muffled groan as he crossed the set, Monsieur Pamplemousse paused to take his bearings. It was hard to locate the exact source of the sound because of the noise from the audience, but it seemed to be coming from somewhere behind Madame Grante's cash desk.

He was about to backtrack when Pommes Frites shot past him, ears facing forward as he homed in on his unseen target. A moment later there was a loud cry: a mixture of alarm and outrage.

Monsieur Pamplemousse's immediate reaction as he joined his friend and mentor was that, apart from being vertical rather than on the slant, Monsieur Leclercq's stance was almost an exact replica of Marcel Aymé's bronze statue outside their apartment block.

The main difference was that, whereas the top half of Marcel Aymé's likeness was permanently embedded in a wall, Monsieur Leclercq's upper torso protruded through a trapdoor in the stage.

'What kept you, Pamplemousse?' he groaned. 'I have been shouting my head off. Where is everyone? And would you kindly remove your hound!'

'*Asseyez-vous!*' Monsieur Pamplemousse called Pommes Frites to heel before turning back to the Director. 'He was only doing what he was trained to do. As Monsieur may remember . . .'

'Yes, yes, I know,' said Monsieur Leclercq impatiently. 'When he was with the Paris *Sûreté* he won the Pierre Armand Golden Bone Trophy for being sniffer dog of the year, but I am not a bone, Pamplemousse, and licking is not the same as sniffing.'

Monsieur Pamplemousse gave Pommes Frites a consoling pat. 'Dogs' saliva is said to be rich in vitamins,' he said.

'It is also rich in *aqua* far from *pura*,' barked the Director. 'It feels as though I have been caught in a sudden downpour outside an abandoned mid-European coal mine.'

'I expect it is all the excitement,' said Monsieur Pamplemousse, resisting the temptation to ask if he was speaking from experience. 'It has probably gone to his head.'

Privately, he had to admit Monsieur Leclercq's face was in a sorry state. Comparisons were odious, of course, but from where he was standing the Director looked as though he could well have been a victim of the wreck of the *Hesperus*. The all over wetness of his visage wasn't helped by the fact that Pommes Frites' ministrations had disturbed much of the carefully applied make-up.

His misgivings communicated themselves to Pommes Frites, who began backing away from the scene while his master hastily reached into his pocket for something with which to repair the damage.

Monsieur Leclercq did a double-take. Drawing back his head as far as it would go, he visibly flinched. 'What is that object you are holding in your hand, Pamplemousse?' he barked.

'Aah!' Monsieur Pamplemousse gave a start.

'It is something Pommes Frites passed on to me.'

'It looks remarkably like an item of ladies' underwear!' exclaimed the Director. 'Something he found discarded under a hedge, no doubt.'

'I have yet to examine it closely,' said Monsieur Pamplemousse, hastily exchanging the offending article for his handkerchief. 'But from my brief knowledge of the owner I have no doubt it is a souvenir of taste and discernment.'

'A *souvenir*?' repeated the Director. 'I will not embarrass you, Pamplemousse, by enquiring as to what event it was celebrating. I very much fear you must have fallen prey to the seamier side of the theatrical profession. It is not as though we are at the end of a long tour of *Les Trois Mousquetaires*, by which time, I am told, such goings-on can become rife.

'As for Pommes Frites, he would be better employed if he had one of those kegs of cognac his colleagues are apt to carry round their necks for use in an emergency.'

'With respect,' said Monsieur Pamplemousse, 'I think you are confusing him with a St Bernard. That is an entirely different breed. The long-haired ones are massive. They are reputed to be related to The Great Pyrénées. Then, of course, there is the short-haired variety . . .' His voice trailed away as he caught the look in the Director's eye.

Seeking refuge in diversionary tactics, he

pushed the movable platform supporting the cash desk to one side. 'Give me your hands, Monsieur.'

'Would that I were able to, Aristide,' groaned Monsieur Leclercq. 'My arms are pinioned to my sides. I am wedged like a bung in a barrel.'

Taking a closer look as he dabbed Monsieur Leclercq's face with his handkerchief, Monsieur Pamplemousse had to agree that, apart from his ears, there was very little to take hold of, and he was reluctant to make use of either one of those, let alone both. Even using all his strength it would be a classic case of the irresistible force up against the immovable object. Something must eventually give.

'I don't understand it,' he said. 'I gave the stage designers precise measurements of your dimensions . . .' He took a step back. 'On the other hand, if I may be so bold, Monsieur, your carbon footprint does seem to have increased more than somewhat during the performance. I didn't take into account the amount of food you would be consuming. I know it is one of the hazards of our calling, but—'

'It is also one of the hazards of what is known as "method acting", Pamplemousse,' groaned the Director. 'I fear I committed a cardinal error by overplaying my part . . .'

'The smell of the greasepaint, the roar of the crowd,' ventured Monsieur Pamplemousse.

'A heady mixture, Aristide,' agreed Monsieur Leclercq. 'I well remember a similar occurrence many years ago . . .'

'Would that be when you were playing the part of Robespierre in a school play?' suggested Monsieur Pamplemousse, knowing full well what the answer would be. The Director lost no time in reminding others of his early triumph whenever he got the chance.

'How *did* you guess, Aristide?' said Monsieur Leclercq. 'I was being pursued by the mob at the time and, as things took a turn for the worse, I sought shelter inside what was meant to be a hole in the ground. As is so often the case with school plays, they try to give everyone a part. It keeps the parents happy. Even at such a tender age, crowd scenes tend to bring out the worst in people, and human nature being what it is there were those who made the most of the situation. I ended up black and blue all over and spent several days in the sanatorium being tended by Matron.'

'Perhaps,' suggested Monsieur Pamplemousse, 'to enlarge on the bung in a barrel analogy, if you could find a suitable purchase for your feet and were able to push in an upward direction, more of you will eventually emerge and that will afford me the opportunity to be of assistance . . .'

'*Impossible!*' exclaimed the Director. 'I have lost the use of my legs.'

Monsieur Pamplemousse was overcome with remorse. Could it be that his words uttered on the spur of the moment in the coach at the behest of others had come true?

'Don't tell me they are broken, Monsieur?' he exclaimed. 'I will have Sister come as soon as she is free. As you may recall, she was playing the part of a district nurse and she is still taking her bow.'

'They are dangling in mid-air, Pamplemousse,' broke in the Director. 'Who knows what may lie beneath them? In this part of the world it might be an underground stream in full spate and I could be sucked into an abyss. I have despatched Rambaud to investigate.'

'Excellent news!' exclaimed Monsieur Pamplemousse, in tones of relief.

'Excellent?' boomed the Director. 'There is nothing excellent about it. The man is a fool.'

'Rambaud *is* a little set in his ways,' admitted Monsieur Pamplemousse. 'Gatekeepers often are. Most of them are ex-army and see things strictly in terms of black and white. He doesn't take kindly to the current trend towards multi-tasking, so it wasn't easy persuading him to take on the job of operating the curtain in addition to being Stage Doorkeeper for the day. Communication can be difficult at the best of times—'

'When you are deprived of the use of your limbs and unable to mime even the simplest request,' said the Director, 'it is well nigh impossible.'

'I can see that . . .' began Monsieur Pamplemousse cautiously. 'In which case . . .'

'I wasn't aware that Rambaud is hard of hearing,' said Monsieur Leclercq. 'It is not something he has ever admitted to on his P27. I was shouting my head off and I wondered why the message was not getting through. I assumed at first my voice was muffled by all the applause from the auditorium, but he kept holding a hand over one ear and giving me the thumbs down sign with the other hand. Then he began pointing to his mouth and finally the message got through. It is my belief he has taught himself to lip read.'

'Perhaps that is why he has acquired a reputation for being so grumpy at times,' said Monsieur Pamplemousse. 'I must make allowances for it when addressing him in future.'

'I shouldn't be too optimistic, Aristide,' said the Director. 'He is far from word perfect. I suggested he remove some of the counterweights on the trap in order to raise it to a reasonable height. Instead of which he brought me a prawn sandwich.'

'Aaah!' Registering the fact that, apart from a few desultory cries, the applause on the other side of the curtain had taken on a more rhythmic quality, verging on that of a hand-clap, Monsieur Pamplemousse couldn't think of anything better to say.

'The whole affair is a *désastre*, Aristide,' exclaimed the Director. 'Not only have I missed all my curtain calls, the press will be waiting, cameras at the ready. At all costs they must be kept at bay. If they catch me like this they will have a field day.'

'I agree it is terrible,' said Monsieur Pamplemousse, 'but your fans are calling for you. It could be your finest hour.'

'They will have to wait, Pamplemousse,' said Monsieur Leclercq firmly. 'All in good time. On no account must they see me like this. Besides, they can't go until I give the waiting buses orders to commence re-embarkation. Until that happens the drivers have strict orders to refuse entry. In the meantime, tell Trigaux to put on a record of the National Anthem—preferably the full version. At least it will keep them quiet.'

Monsieur Pamplemousse stared at the Director. A generous person in many ways, vanity was often his downfall. At such times his complete and utter selfishness was hard to credit.

He drew a deep breath. Someone had to tell him.

'Monsieur,' he began, 'you are absolutely right, of course . . . but you have your public to consider. You cannot—you *must* not let them down. Audiences can be very fickle when roused and it would not be in your own interests. Nor would it be in accord with the best theatrical traditions. The show must go on, come what may.'

'But the show has finished, Aristide—'

'The show has never finished until the theatre is emptied and the audience has gone home,' persisted Monsieur Pamplemousse. 'If we raise the curtain now it will look as though it is meant. Many will consider it a stroke of genius.'

Monsieur Leclercq hesitated. 'Do you really think so, Aristide?'

'Provided you really are well and truly wedged, Monsieur, I am sure of it. It is not as though you are about to plunge to your death. Think of the chaos that would cause.'

The Director shuddered. 'Quite frankly, Aristide, I would rather not. On the other hand . . .'

Sensing a momentary hesitation, Monsieur Pamplemousse pressed home his point. 'Audiences are always disappointed when the star doesn't take a bow. They feel insulted.'

The Director visibly pulled himself together. Had his arms not been pinioned, he would almost certainly have slipped into his Napoleonic mode. Instead, he made do by cocking his head to one side, taking in the growing restiveness on the other side of the curtain.

'You are absolutely right, Aristide. Tell Rambaud to raise the curtain.'

'That won't be easy,' said Monsieur Pamplemousse dubiously. 'As it is, he doesn't know whether he is coming or going.'

'Nonsense!' boomed Monsieur Leclercq. 'The curtain is electrically powered. All he has to do is press a button.'

'It isn't as simple as that, I fear,' said Monsieur Pamplemousse. 'Rambaud is a glutton for sticking to the rules. He has his written instructions.'

'Then you must override them,' barked the Director. 'Tell him it is an order from on high. Quick! There is not a moment to be lost.'

Fearing the worst, Monsieur Pamplemousse dashed towards the wings with Pommes Frites hard on his heels.

'Ah,' growled Rambaud as he drew near. 'Don't tell me 'e wants another of them prawn sandwiches.'

He broke off as Monsieur Pamplemousse took matters into his own hands and brushed past him. '*Mon Dieu!* What are you doing? That's my job, that is.' He held a sheet of paper aloft. 'I 'as my instructions. Raise the curtain once at the start and lower it at the end . . .'

Rambaud was about to let forth in no uncertain terms on the rights and wrongs of the matter, but he was too late.

For a brief moment as the curtain began to rise there was a hush and then, as the audience took in the scene on stage, they instinctively

66

rose to their feet as one and burst into spontaneous applause.

Apart from feeling vindicated, Monsieur Pamplemousse was momentarily overcome by the warmth of their approval, but it quickly evaporated.

What he had not bargained on was the reaction of the members of the press corps. Never ones to miss a scoop when it was handed to them on a plate, they made a concerted dash down the aisles. Cameras at the ready, they swarmed onto the stage like a pack of hungry locusts jockeying for position.

In a matter of seconds, the Director disappeared behind a sea of bodies and flashing lights. It struck Monsieur Pamplemousse that they had no need to hurry; Monsieur Leclercq wouldn't be going anywhere for some time to come, but the thought had barely entered his mind when he felt himself being pushed to one side.

Seizing the initiative for once, or perhaps it was simply a reflex action brought on by the fact that his territory had been invaded and needed protecting, Rambaud reached up and, after switching on a warning bell to indicate the safety curtain was about to be lowered, began clearing the stage, uttering dire warnings as to the fate of anyone who had the misfortune to get in its way.

'Several tonnes, it weighs,' he announced. 'If 'e lands on any of your 'eads, it'll be enough to crack them open like a load of walnuts at Christmas.'

It did the trick. As quickly as they had arrived, the members of the press beat a hasty retreat. They'd had their moment. No doubt the combined efforts would find their way into the papers on the morrow. Quite how Monsieur Leclercq would view them in the cold light of day was another matter. It would depend a lot on how the headline writers dealt with the subject. It might be grist to their mill.

While making good their escape, the more enterprising among the press corps began taking reaction shots of the audience.

Monsieur Pamplemousse was about to rejoin the Director when he caught sight of Corby. His face was a study in mixed emotions. Seeing one of the photographers approach him, he looked for a moment as though he was about to make a grab for the man's camera.

After a brief struggle, clearly realising he would be outnumbered, he thought better of it and pulled himself free. Looking as black as thunder, he made a dash for the stage door, almost knocking Rambaud flying in the process.

'Not one of your better ideas, Aristide, I fear,' boomed the Director as Monsieur Pamplemousse drew near. 'Did you see the expression on Corby's face? He has obviously taken umbrage. I strongly suspect he saw himself in the part I was playing and assumed I was making a mockery of him. He couldn't wait to escape.'

'Do you think people recognise themselves as others see them?' asked Monsieur Pamplemousse. 'I have heard it said on good authority that it seldom happens.'

'In this instance,' said Monsieur Leclercq, 'I suspect the answer is "yes, they do". I fear the worst!'

'But you were magnificent,' said Monsieur Pamplemousse. 'He can hardly fault your performance. He only had to listen to the applause.'

The Director shook his head sadly. 'Therein lies the rub, Aristide. I fear it was a little too good. Once again, it was the smell of the greasepaint! It does something to me. It is like sampling a glass of Margaux '45. It sends the blood coursing through my veins.'

'I am afraid it is a comparison I am unable to make,' said Monsieur Pamplemousse.

'You mean you have never been backstage before?' exclaimed Monsieur Leclercq.

'I have never sampled a Margaux '45,' said Monsieur Pamplemousse.

The Director stared at him as though doubting such a thing were possible. 'Make no mistake about it, Pamplemousse. If Corby makes a bad report, sales of *Le Guide* in the United States will plummet still further. Everything possible needs to be done to placate him. We must contact him before he gets in touch with his lawyers.'

'We?' echoed Monsieur Pamplemousse warily.

Monsieur Leclercq sighed. 'I trust you are not going to be difficult, Pamplemousse.

'I used the word "we" loosely,' he added hastily, reading the other's thoughts. 'I know I can rely on you, Aristide. But I shall be right behind you. For the time being, until I have secured my release and received the all-clear from Sister, it will be metaphorically speaking of course.'

'Corby is not staying with you?' asked Monsieur Pamplemousse.

'He was very insistent on making his own arrangements,' said Monsieur Leclercq. 'I must say at the time I was somewhat relieved. It avoided any possible accusations of his doing me a favour. It's the kind of the thing the press would pick up on like a shot.'

'And he didn't leave you a forwarding address?'

The Director shook his head. 'Clearly, he didn't wish to tell me and I was reluctant to press the point. He is a strange mixture. On the surface he is inclined to be a trifle tetchy, but beneath it all he is surprisingly modest. He only agreed to be here provided no one else knew and I paid in cash. He jumped at the chance when I agreed.'

'I will telephone the local police straight away,' said Monsieur Pamplemousse. 'They should be able to help.'

The Director went pale at the thought. 'That is the last thing you must do. If Corby gets to hear of it, it will only exacerbate matters and risk negating the whole operation.'

'Perhaps he is already on his way back to the airport . . .' said Monsieur Pamplemousse dubiously.

'In that case,' said the Director, 'you must intercept him. You are an ex-detective. With Pommes Frites' help it should be a simple matter. There is not a moment to be lost. He was driven down here by car, but at his request it was dismissed. I think he wanted to make his own arrangements. Perhaps see a little of the country while he was over here.'

'But . . .' began Monsieur Pamplemousse. 'I have my wife to think of. Doucette and I drove down together . . .'

'Doing nothing is not an option, Aristide,' said Monsieur Leclercq firmly. 'It is an *"Estragon"* situation and there is no time to be lost. Corby must be placated at all costs.'

The Director's use of *Le Guide*'s code word denoting an emergency underlined the seriousness of the situation. It was not a word he used lightly.

A thought struck Monsieur Pamplemousse. 'Perhaps the girl knows where he is?'

Monsieur Leclercq managed a beam. 'There you are, Aristide,' he said. 'I knew you wouldn't let me down. You have a clue

71

already. Correct me if I am wrong, but in your previous occupation was it not known as a case of *cherchez la femme?*

'Find Corby and you shall have a bottle of Margaux '45. I think I have one left in my cellar.'

Monsieur Pamplemousse felt sorely tempted to ask if that could be confirmed in writing, but since it was clearly impossible he refrained. Anyway, it was hardly the moment.

'As for Pommes Frites,' continued the Director magnanimously, 'I have every faith in his olfactory powers. To use a phrase one often hears bandied about these days . . . May the force go with him.

'And Pamplemousse . . .'

'Monsieur?'

'In the meantime, never lose sight of *Le Guide*'s motto—the three As: *Action, Accord, Anonymat.*'

Monsieur Pamplemousse stifled his response. Action was undoubtedly possible. Accord depended a great deal on matters outside his control. As for keeping the whole thing anonymous, he had his doubts.

'You must convey to Pommes Frites that, should he prove successful in his endeavours, a visit to *Boucherie Lamartine* will not come amiss. I shall have great pleasure in making sure they afford him *carte blanche.*'

Pommes Frites' tail began to wag at the mere mention of Paris's premier purveyor of beef. He licked his lips. Clearly, when combined with other key words his brain had already registered, whatever it was he had done to upset his master's boss was now a thing of the past.

In his book there was but one simple, time-honoured way to express his thanks.

The Director's bellow of rage was still ringing in Monsieur Pamplemousse's ears as he headed for the stage door with Pommes Frites at his heels.

At least it brought others running to Monsieur Leclercq's aid, diverting attention from their sudden departure.

Rambaud was back at his post. For some reason best known to himself, he was looking unusually cheerful.

'The American?' He put two fingers to the side of his nose and gave Monsieur Pamplemousse a wink. 'He had a car already waiting for 'im, but I've no idea where 'e went to. At least . . .'

'Out with it,' said Monsieur Pamplemousse. Sensing a tongue-loosing situation, he reached for his wallet.

'Well,' said Rambaud, pocketing a €50 note. 'Since you ask, Monsieur Pamplemousse, I did 'ave a chat with the driver and 'e mentioned the word Deauville at one point, but don't say I said so.

'As for the girl . . .'

'The girl?' repeated Monsieur Pamplemousse.

'The one that was sitting a few rows behind 'im before 'e made a break for it.' Rambaud gave a cackle. 'I reckon 'e's in for a bad time when she catches up with him. *If* she ever does. It took me a while to find 'er a taxi on account of what you might call the American gentleman's generosity, but she made it worth my while when she did.'

Monsieur Pamplemousse stared at Rambaud. It was no wonder he was looking so cheerful.

A little voice reminded him of a quotation his English friend, Mr Pickering, was fond of using.

Success in his mission would be what the famous lexicographer Dr Johnson would have called 'the triumph of optimism over experience.'

CHAPTER FOUR

'I thought it was too good to last,' said Doucette, as they drove into the vast parking area outside the *gare* in Deauville.

'Don't worry, Couscous. It won't be for long.' Monsieur Pamplemousse brought his *Deux Chevaux* to rest in a space opposite the main entrance. 'The sooner I get started the sooner we will be together again.'

Leaving his wife in the car, he hurried into

the booking hall, returning shortly afterwards armed with a ticket.

'I've booked you first class on the 17.07. It's due in at the Gare St Lazare just after 19.00.'

He waved aside her protests. 'Have it on *Le Guide* and travel in comfort. It is the least Monsieur Leclercq can do.'

'Why does it always have to be you?' said Doucette. 'Why can't he go to the police like anyone else?'

'Because . . .' said Monsieur Pamplemousse. 'You know how he hates any kind of bad publicity, and in this case he has a point. Anyway, they wouldn't be interested. It isn't a matter of life and death. Corby isn't on the missing persons list—yet.'

Doucette gave a sigh. 'I know.'

'The worst scenario would be if he heads back to Paris and catches a plane for home.'

'How about Interpol? Don't they deal with that kind of thing?'

Monsieur Pamplemousse looked dubious. 'He hasn't committed a crime. They have their hands full dealing with terrorists and known criminals. By all accounts, their annual budget isn't a great deal bigger than the amount the New York Police Department spends in one week. Unless Corby is using a stolen passport or has a criminal record, they're not going to lose any sleep over it. Besides, it would need a request from the appropriate body and that wouldn't go down too well with the Director.

For the time being, Pommes Frites and I are on our own.

'I checked at the booking office and the last train out of here was at 16.42. He wouldn't have made it in time to catch that, and he's certainly nowhere to be seen.

'I doubt if he is very far away. If he's in Deauville, he shouldn't have much trouble getting a room. The season hasn't really started yet so it's probably mostly Parisian wives and their offspring staking out the territory before their husbands join them for a long weekend.'

'Armed with nannies to look after the children in the evening, leaving them free to follow other pursuits,' said Doucette. 'That's what bothers me. I know you.'

'Couscous! How could you?'

'Easily,' said Doucette.

Monsieur Pamplemousse glanced at his watch. 'I think it's time we made a move.'

Having validated Doucette's ticket, he led her along the platform towards the first two coaches of the Paris train, keeping an eye out all the while for any sign of Corby, but it was almost entirely full of families homeward bound. He would have stood out like a sore thumb.

'It's been a wonderful day, Aristide,' said Doucette, giving him a hug. 'I'm very proud of you. Take care.'

'We will catch up on everything when I get

back,' he promised. 'After all the work I have put in I think we've earned the right to some time off together.' He was about to add that if all went well they might be able to celebrate the occasion in a grand way, but no sooner had the notion entered his mind than he thought better of it.

For the time being, it was best to keep quiet about the Director's promises and content himself with dreams of being home again with his own modest cellar.

Waving goodbye, he returned to the car in order to make certain he had all the things needed to tide him over the next day or two; he didn't picture it being any longer than that.

Both *Le Guide*'s issue case and his own travel bag were still in place. He went through the latter quickly to make sure it still contained a change of clothing, along with various basic items of toiletry. Knowing Doucette, he felt sure everything would have been washed, ironed, and replenished during his unusually long spell at home, but it was better to be safe than sorry.

Opening up *Le Guide*'s case, he scanned the contents, marvelling as always at the Director's attention to detail. From its early beginnings in the Founder's day, when it contained little more than the bare necessities in the way of emergency rations, bandages and a bottle of iodine, all contained in the pannier bag of Monsieur Hippolyte Duval's Michaux boneshaker bicycle, it now boasted practically every possible item of equipment necessary to sustain life under the most adverse conditions.

To give him his due, Monsieur Leclercq wasn't one to stint in such matters and he was forever updating it.

Removing a pair of Leitz Trinovid binoculars, Monsieur Pamplemousse closed the lid, then made sure Pommes Frites' king-size inflatable kennel and cylinder of compressed air were also at the ready, along with a supply of biscuits well within their consume-by date. It was just as well. As far as he could recall, *chiens* were *interdit* in most of Deauville's major hotels.

Suitably reassured, he locked the boot, attached an ATTENTION! CHIEN MÉCHANT. MAITRE FÉROCE card to the windscreen to guard against possible intruders and, with Pommes Frites at his side, set off to explore Deauville on foot.

More than anything else, he needed a strong dose of fresh sea air. So much had happened that day, his mind was still in a whirl. In current phraseology it needed a quantum leap to make the change from the land of make-believe to the real world outside.

It was several years since he had last been in Deauville, and then it had been on a routine visit for *Le Guide*, which hadn't left much time for sightseeing. In any case, anonymity being an important element in the Director's operation, it was against company policy to visit the same area too often or to linger overlong once the report had been completed.

Today was an exception, of course, but provided he kept clear of the last places he'd reported on, he should be reasonably safe. Single men dining alone were often objects of suspicion, a man and his dog usually passed muster.

He could see the Director's problem; his own and that of his colleagues too, come to that. One way or another they were all affected. It would be a crying shame if Corby vented his spleen on *Le Guide* to such an extent that the day's efforts came to naught.

If his quarry were spending the night anywhere near the Leclercqs' summer home, his most likely choice would be either Deauville or Trouville. In that particular part of Normandy all roads led to the Côte Fleurie and its twin resorts on opposite banks of the River Touques. An added plus from his point of view was the fact that, being on the coast, unless Corby backtracked, his options for moving on elsewhere at that time of the day were strictly limited.

Deauville, with its Grand Hotels, its two racecourses—one for flat racing, the other for steeplechases, along with the world famous boardwalk—struck him as being the better bet of the two.

Trouville may have been the first on the

scene, but it was on the wrong side of the track for many people; ideal for building sandcastles and other more plebeian seaside pursuits, but somehow he couldn't picture it holding much appeal for Corby.

Apart from the vast marina, which was still growing if the row upon row of moored yachts was anything to go by, Deauville was much as Monsieur Pamplemousse remembered it.

Making use of the binoculars, he scanned the area beyond it, towards the casino and the Thalassotherapie. Perhaps not surprisingly given the time of day, the former looked deserted. As for the health centre, that was another area he couldn't picture holding much appeal for Corby.

There again, having only observed him from afar, as it were, what did he know about his likes and dislikes? Apart from hearsay, what did anyone really know?

Sensing Pommes Frites prick up his ears, Monsieur Pamplemousse lowered the glasses and hastily moved to one side just in time to avoid being run down by a rubber-tyred tourist train doing a round of sights. Laden with small children, it was probably their last treat of the day.

Giving the tiny passengers a passing wave as they disappeared around a corner, Monsieur Pamplemousse resumed his walk. Lost in thought, he headed towards the beach area.

Something about the whole affair didn't

quite gel. Why, for instance, was Corby so insistent about doing his own thing? He didn't strike Monsieur Pamplemousse as being a shrinking violet; by all accounts, he was very much the reverse. Presumably, he would also forfeit any claim he might have on his extraneous expenses being taken care of by *Le Guide*, which again seemed out of character. Perhaps he had a secret assignation, which would explain his behaviour when the girl turned up out of the blue . . .

Although he kept catching tantalising glimpses of the sea, it was further away than he had bargained for, and in the end they had to follow a zigzag route past a pony club and a miniature clock golf course before the *Planche* came into view.

Running the entire length of what in most seaside towns would have been a paved esplanade, the boardwalk was lined on the inland side with white huts, each with a sign outside commemorating a visit by a member of the film industry to the festival held each September; film stars, producers, directors . . .

Not only was it a unique way of helping visitors remember where they had left their belongings, it was also a tourist attraction in its own right; as famous in its way as the terrace of the Café de la Paix in Paris.

Who was it that said if you stopped by the latter for a leisurely coffee someone you knew would eventually pass by? Perhaps one of its famous habitués—there had been so many over the years—Victor Hugo, Conan Doyle, Oscar Wilde . . . it was hard to remember.

It would save a lot of time if the same held true of Deauville's boardwalk and Corby just happened to stroll past.

Raising the binoculars, he scanned the serried ranks of red and blue sunshades erected in military fashion across the vast sandy bay. Despite the sunshine, the majority remained unopened. In a few weeks' time, when the season began in earnest, it would be a different story.

A few hardy kite flyers had made it as far as the water's edge, but that was all.

Visitors to Deauville's boardwalk were mostly people who went there to see and be seen; the minority were those with memories of Claude Lelouch's film *Un Homme et Une Femme*, and were simply enjoying a nostalgic day out seeing the setting for real. On the whole, neither category believed in total immersion.

Pommes Frites had no such qualms. At a nod from his master he headed off down the beach as fast as he could go.

Monsieur Pamplemousse watched him enter the sea without a second's hesitation and, given the fact that he had no desire to follow suit, focused his mind instead on more mundane matters. Having missed out on the barbecue, and with his stomach reminding him that it was a long time since he had last eaten, he opted for an open-air café nearby.

Glass panels ran along the front of the main eating area, presumably for the benefit of the older clientele, many of whom looked as though they had spent the morning in a beauty parlour and needed protection from any prevailing wind.

Ensconced along the top of it, a row of sparrows were on the lookout for anything that was going, prepared to pounce on tables as soon as there was the slightest sign of them being vacated. He didn't fancy their chances very much. Most of the occupants looked as though they had been there for ever.

The nearest one in particular gave him a very unfriendly look when she saw him hovering in the entrance. She was clutching what appeared to be a very small dog. At first sight it looked like a Chihuahua wearing a diamond encrusted collar and matching jacket embroidered with the words 'Phoenix, Arizona'. A closer look revealed it was a hand muff. Presumably what felt like a warm summer's day in Deauville seemed like winter to someone from that part of the world.

Opting for a small table just inside the entrance, where he could keep an eye on both Pommes Frites and the passers-by, Monsieur Pamplemousse sought shelter from his neighbour's icy gaze behind a large menu.

Taking stock of his surroundings as best he

could, he realised Doucette's summing up was not far short of the truth.

There was hardly another man in sight. Everywhere he looked the customers were predominantly female, either alone or with their children and their minders. Most of the latter looked as though they were busy packing up for the day.

At a nearby table, one of them, obviously running late, was hastily dissecting a steak on behalf of a small figure kicking up a fuss at the sight of some spinach on the side of its plate.

It was hard to tell what sex the child was behind its Karl Lagerfeld sunglasses, and its mother was far too busy talking to a friend at the next table to care one way or the other.

All the action appeared to be concentrated at the far end of the restaurant. Mobile phones were very much in evidence, and from the way they were being held, lips close to the business end, the air was thick with intrigue. Thoughts of an early bedtime clearly weren't confined to those mewling and puking in their nurses' arms.

Ordering a plate of *crevettes grises* and a glass of the local draught cider, Monsieur Pamplemousse sat back to make the most of what was left of the sunshine. Half of him regretted Doucette wasn't there to enjoy it with him, the other half—and privately he had to admit it was the greater of the two—felt relieved because he needed space to think.

For a brief moment he toyed with the idea of putting through a call to the train, but she so rarely had her own mobile switched on it would have been a pointless exercise.

The Director's words came back to him: '*Cherchez la femme.*' He had a point. Find the lady and she might lead him to the man.

Perhaps it was something he could set Pommes Frites to work on when he returned from his swim. The girl must be somewhere around; probably not far away if the truth be known, and he still had the garment she had given him. It would be a good exercise for Pommes Frites' talents.

His musings were interrupted by the arrival of his order and, on the spur of the moment, he took out his camera, switched it to PLAY, and set it to the shot he had taken of the group on the Leclercqs' patio.

Holding it up, he shaded the screen with his other hand so that the waiter could see the picture clearly. It was a wild card, but he might as well play it; anything was worth a try.

'The man on the left, drinking from a large glass containing something dark . . . would he have been here earlier this afternoon?'

The waiter peered at the picture. 'In this job,' he said, 'everybody begins to look the same after a while. If I might borrow Monsieur's binoculars . . .'

Reading the signs for the third time that day, Monsieur Pamplemousse removed a €50 note from his wallet and laid it casually on the table.

The waiter flicked the surface with his napkin. Clearly the disappearing note trick was one he had perfected over the years. In its way, it was poetry in motion.

'If Monsieur will allow me to borrow the camera, I will ask around.'

Monsieur Pamplemousse passed it to him, took a long draught of cider, and set to work on his snack.

His normal *modus operandi* automatically kicked in.

The *crevettes* were a pale shade of pink, still glisteningly fresh from the morning's catch—it was probably one up to Trouville, which boasted a thriving fish market. The finger bowl had a slice of lemon floating in the water; there was a generous helping of mayonnaise in another bowl, and the slices of baguette in a separate basket felt satisfyingly crisp to the touch; definitely the second baking of the day, perhaps even the third or fourth.

It was little wonder the sparrows were queuing up. A prime example of the true meaning of the phrase 'pecking order', the prizes went to the bold and the fleet of wing.

Glancing around, it was easy to spot their human equivalents.

It had to do with the way they were sitting. It wasn't simply a case of the swinging leg syndrome; it also had to do with their position when at rest. His colleague Truffert would have had a field day. Having spent some time working on cruise ships when he was in the Merchant Navy, he was an expert on such matters, maintaining that the position of a person's legs could speak volumes.

The butter was soft but not runny; it wasn't *Echiré*, but . . . He spread a little on a portion of bread. It might lack the other's nutty aroma, but it ran a close second.

Automatically reaching down for the concealed pocket in his right trouser leg, where he kept a notebook permanently at the ready, he remembered all too late he was wearing his best suit and converted the movement into adjusting the napkin.

In the beginning it was hard to gauge the reaction the waiter was getting. A cursory glance was clearly enough for most of the customers. Others simply looked the other way as though suspecting him of trying to sell them something.

Then, as he approached some tables in the far corner of the restaurant, there was a distinct change of mood. The first person he approached nudged her companion and together they took a closer look at the camera. Following a brief word with the waiter, they glanced towards Monsieur Pamplemousse.

It was encouraging to say the least. Proof, if proof were needed, that on the whole the fair sex were better than men at remembering faces. They picked up on the details. His spirits rose as the waiter moved on, and one after another others began acting in like manner.

Obviously the man had struck oil. It was like a chain reaction. Some even terminated a phone call they had been making in order to take a closer look, first at the picture, then at him. Others reached for their handbag.

What were the symptoms Truffert had described? According to him, if you came across a lady passenger on the sun deck sitting with her knees pressed tightly together and her feet splayed widely apart, you could bet your bottom dollar there was but one thing uppermost on her mind, and it wasn't the distant horizon (which did not necessarily mean she would give you the number of her cabin just like that). On the other hand, those whose legs were double crossed, often misconstrued as indicating a no-go area, were generally speaking a dead cert, unless of course they belonged to someone so old they were stuck like it. The woman just across from him looked as though she came into that category.

His attention was momentarily diverted by the return of Pommes Frites. Fresh from his dip in the sea, to Monsieur Pamplemousse's secret delight he shook himself dry over the child with the dark glasses, producing another bout of childish wrath.

For reasons best known to themselves, those

at the far end of the café became even more excited.

Spurred on by their varied reactions and thinking to maximise the situation by making full use of his friend and mentor's talents, Monsieur Pamplemousse removed Amber's present from his trouser pocket, shook it in a circular fashion in order to remove the creases, and presented it to Pommes Frites for inspection.

Brief though the manoeuvre had been, it clearly hadn't passed unnoticed. Truffert would have had a field day as legs and knees went into overdrive.

Once again it was a long shot, but Monsieur Pamplemousse had every faith in Pommes Frites' powers. A few seconds of quality time with an object were usually more than sufficient to set all his faculties racing. Words such as *chercher* and *trouver*, spurring him on to seek and find the object's owner, were entirely unnecessary. Indeed, he would have been mortally offended had his master given voice to them, for it would have demonstrated a total lack of confidence in his abilities; abilities honed to perfection over the years.

It was wonderful the way bloodhounds were able to pick up and follow a trail that was often several days old. It was on record that they could even pick up the scent after their quarry attempted to escape by swimming a river.

Not for a moment did it occur to Monsieur

Pamplemousse that for once his own mind and that of Pommes Frites might be working at cross-purposes.

Consequently, he was all the more taken aback when the latter took hold of the object in his mouth and hurried off without so much as a by-your-leave.

It was an unprecedented departure from the norm and once again he found himself automatically reaching inside his trouser pocket, this time for the silent dog whistle he kept there for use in an emergency.

Once again, he stopped short. In any case, by then Pommes Frites was already showing the garment to the lady across the way.

Monsieur Pamplemousse regretted having given up his camera. The look on her face as she eyed it was yet another Cartier-Bresson opportunity gone to waste.

Pommes Frites hurried on his way, following the route previously taken by the waiter. It had been a bad start, but instinct told him better things lay ahead, ready and waiting, and sure enough, not even Charles Aznavour at his peak could have wished for a better reception than the one that greeted him when he arrived at the far end.

Monsieur Pamplemousse waved in vain.

Misinterpreting his signal, the waiter materialised at his side. Clutching a handful of cards and pieces of paper, he gave an admiring wink as he spread them out across the table. 'I think most of them got the message, Monsieur.

'I wouldn't mind a couple of prints myself some time,' he added, returning the camera.

'But . . .' Monsieur Pamplemousse was about to say he had no idea what the man was talking about when he caught sight of the screen. Someone must have been playing with the buttons for, instead of showing the group on the patio, the picture on display had reverted to the one he'd taken of the girl and Pommes Frites in the changing room.

His heart sank as he riffled through the small pile of papers. From a cursory glance they appeared to be covered in telephone numbers; mobiles, mostly. Some were written in pencil, others scribbled in ink. Kisses accompanied the vast majority of them.

He was on the point of asking the waiter to make out the bill as quickly as possible when he thought better of it. While his mind had been focused on more immediate matters, he had been vaguely aware of some kind of minor commotion on the far side of the restaurant, but it seemed to have died down. What did bother him was the fact that Pommes Frites was nowhere to be seen. There was a definite change in the atmosphere: a sense of expectancy intermingled with signs of growing impatience on the part of the other diners.

In order to gain time while awaiting developments, Monsieur Pamplemousse began toying with the remaining *crevettes*, examining each and every one with the air of a connoisseur before dipping it into the bowl of mayonnaise.

After each mouthful he dabbed at his lips with the napkin for as long as was decently possible, and when he had milked that to the full, he tried telephoning Doucette. As he had surmised, he couldn't get through, so he held a lengthy conversation with an imaginary voice at the other end, accompanying it with suitable gestures.

So engrossed was he in the ploy he totally failed to notice some new arrivals at his side.

'I was walking along the boardwalk looking for a certain person,' said a familiar voice, 'when guess who I bumped into? Pommes Frites—up to his rear-end in the sand. You should have seen the way he jumped when I gave his tail a tweak.'

Monsieur Pamplemousse mimed terminating his call. Never before had he been so relieved to see a familiar face.

'It's a pity I wasn't there with my camera,' he said. 'I could have added it to my collection. It would have been a case of the biter bit.'

'Perhaps this little lot will do instead,' said Amber. 'I managed to rescue them before they got covered up. I don't know how far the tide comes in.'

Lifting the flap on her shoulder bag she withdrew a handful of lingerie. 'I'm most impressed. Even in his heyday Charles

Aznavour could hardly have struck a richer seam, and you haven't even sung a note. Or have you?'

Monsieur Pamplemousse shook his head and pointed to the pile of messages on the table. 'I have enough notes to last me.'

'Does this kind of thing happen often?' asked Amber, as he hastily concealed them as best he could under the menu, along with Pommes Frites' haul.

'My bottom drawer is full to overflowing,' said Monsieur Pamplemousse dryly.

'May you be forgiven,' said Amber. 'That's a dreadful pun. It seems to me it's a good thing I came along when I did.'

Monsieur Pamplemousse looked down at the face peering up at him. 'I can't understand what came over him.'

Pommes Frites started to wag his tail, then decided against it. He had been wearing his pleased expression; the one he kept in reserve for those occasions when he had completed what was in his opinion a job well done.

Still on cloud nine following his first taste of stardom and anxious to show his appreciation other than with a mere lick, which would dry off in no time at all, he had been racking his brain for a suitable gift; the human equivalent of a bone.

The answer had literally landed on the end of his nose.

Since his master was still carrying the object

around in his pocket it must mean a great deal to him. And if he was prepared to hand it over, that could mean only one thing. He wanted others to see how lucky he was.

Speaking personally, he couldn't understand the need for such items. It was yet another strange example of human behaviour. They were the first things they put on in the morning and on the whole the last things they took off at night. He had even seen them hanging up in shop windows.

Sensing sympathetic vibrations on the far side of the café, pulsations that had grown even more intense since he returned from his dip in the ocean, and presuming his master wanted them to be shown to all and sundry, that was where he eventually ended up.

Even so, he was ill-prepared for the reception that was granted him. With scarcely a discernible wriggle from the owners, who as a body carried on talking as though nothing untoward was happening, table after table yielded up its quota of spoils. They showered down on his head like leaves in an autumn gale.

Mission accomplished, he had gathered them up as quickly as possible and hurried off with them, intent on finding a safe hiding place before anyone had second thoughts.

Amber bent down to remove a strand of something black caught between two of his front teeth.

'Someone's token gesture,' she said, holding it up for him to see. 'Aren't you the lucky one!'

Pommes Frites eyed her gratefully.

'I would rather not know,' said Monsieur Pamplemousse.

'There's a first time for everything,' said Amber. 'Let's hope it doesn't become a habit.'

'I'm sure he meant well,' said Monsieur Pamplemousse. 'Pommes Frites never does anything without a good reason, but it isn't always easy to read his mind.

'If I may?' Raising the menu, he plucked the cause of the misunderstanding from the pile and slipped it back into his pocket.

'Actions speak louder than words,' said Amber. 'I am very touched.'

'And I have a feeling,' said Monsieur Pamplemousse, 'you should return the rest to your bag as quickly as possible. They are attracting rather a lot of attention.'

'Aren't you going to try returning them to their rightful owners?' asked Amber.

'Would you?' asked Monsieur Pamplemousse. 'Half of them are covered in sand anyway and I doubt if they have any name tags. There isn't room on most of them.'

Following Monsieur Pamplemousse's advice, Amber did as he suggested, then withdrew a small compact, flipped it open, and held the mirror up to her face.

'I see what you mean. I thought I could feel a tingling sensation all down my spine. If looks could kill . . .'

'Winged daggers aimed with intent,' said Monsieur Pamplemousse.

'Hell hath no fury . . .' said Amber.

'And we are considerably outnumbered,' said Monsieur Pamplemousse.

Amber snapped her compact shut, then reached over and speared the last of the *crevettes* with a fork.

'May I? I'm starving. Do you have any ideas for Plan B? Like, how do we get out of here in one piece?'

'An early dinner for three?' suggested Monsieur Pamplemousse.

Pommes Frites' tail began to wag, distributing a certain amount of dried sand as it did.

Having waited patiently while his master paid the bill, and giving the table on the other side of the entrance a wide berth—a totally unnecessary manoeuvre, as the occupant had long since departed—he joined in the dash for the boardwalk, pausing for a moment to look back when they reached it, as though daring anyone to follow in their wake.

For the time being at least there were no takers.

CHAPTER FIVE

As a precautionary measure, Monsieur Pamplemousse chose a more direct, but considerably less populated, route back to his car; inland along rue Raspail, then left into the Avenue de la République. He had no wish to be stalked by some female harbouring a supposed grievance and out for revenge; still less a whole horde of them.

They were not out of the woods yet. No doubt mobiles were already being put to good use; descriptions issued. If the look of hatred in their eyes was anything to go by and they connected him to his *Deux Chevaux,* there was no knowing what damage they might inflict. It would be slashed tyres after dark at the very least, and then he really would be in the soup. He decided to keep his eyes peeled ready to take evasive action if need be.

'This part of Deauville is very un-French,' Amber broke into his thoughts. 'More like Main Street USA. Somewhere in the US Bible Belt, I guess . . . like . . . I don't know . . .'

'Phoenix, Arizona?' hazarded Monsieur Pamplemousse. _

'I have never been there,' she said, 'but I can imagine. Except the streets would be even wider, four or five lanes in each direction probably, but they couldn't be any straighter

97

than these.'

'It was ahead of its time.'

'I tell you one difference for sure—all those generals you name your streets after: de Gaulle, Leclerc, Hoche . . . they're much more romantic. Better than E14th or whatever any time.

'And the quaint architecture too . . .'

'Seaside Norman,' said Monsieur Pamplemousse. 'Belle Epoque with a touch of Alsace-Lorraine thrown in for good measure. Deauville didn't evolve; most of it was put together from a kit of parts over a period of three years in the late eighteen hundreds when the Duc de Morny began developing it as a weekend retreat for rich Parisians.

'Being Napoleon III's half-brother was a big help. It enabled him to persuade the railway company to open a branch line, making it only four cigars distance away from Paris, for those who timed their journeys that way.

'In time, Deauville acquired the nickname of being Paris's 21st *arrondissement*, which gave it a head start over the South of France, and having miraculously survived two world wars more or less intact, it hasn't lost its air of faded grandeur.'

'You sound just like a guidebook,' said Amber.

'I happen to work for one,' said Monsieur Pamplemousse. 'Ask me another.'

'Apart from fleeing all those predatory ladies

and our having dinner together, what else do you have in mind?'

'I'm trying to track down our guest of honour ...'

'Jay?' She looked at him thoughtfully. 'That makes two of us. What do you reckon are the chances of finding him?'

'If he is in Deauville, it shouldn't be too difficult, but we need to work quickly in case he moves on.'

'What then?'

'France may not be as vast as America,' said Monsieur Pamplemousse. 'But it's still a big country by European standards: 550,000 square kilometres, a population of 60 million plus, and nearly 40,000 towns and villages in which to hide away. It really depends on how serious he is about wanting to be alone.'

'He's serious,' said Amber. 'Garbo had nothing on him.'

Monsieur Pamplemousse gave her a sidelong glance. She sounded as though she meant it.

'You know what he said the last time I asked him what his plans were?'

Monsieur Pamplemousse shook his head. He was in no mood for conundrums.

'Read the tea-leaves, honey.'

They walked along in silence for a moment or two, each busy with their own thoughts.

'What we need,' said Amber, 'is some kind of road map.'

Monsieur Pamplemousse put the 'we' on hold for the time being. 'You're welcome to borrow any of mine,' he said. 'I have a whole stack of them in the car.'

'I mean a *Plan* with a capital P,' said Amber. 'The kind of road map George Bush used to have for the Middle East.'

'I don't want to sound sceptical,' said Monsieur Pamplemousse, 'but—'

'Look where it didn't get him? I know.'

Monsieur Pamplemousse paused while Pommes Frites investigated something in the gutter. He seized the opportunity to look around. Everything seemed quiet enough and there was no one else in sight.

'Forgive my asking,' he said. 'It's none of my business—'

'But what's between Jay and me? Not what you're probably thinking. He's in denial about that side of things. His proclivities lie elsewhere. To put it bluntly, he swings whichever way the wind blows, and that's not my scene.'

For no special reason he could put into words, Monsieur Pamplemousse had to admit he felt glad.

'How did you meet up with him in the first place?'

'I was working for an American company, Waist Disposals Inc. They specialise in over-extended girth problems. I started off modelling for their "before and after" adverts and that led to helping with the deportment classes.

'Jay was a dropout from "Overeaters Anonymous". He thought he would give us a try. We didn't get very far with his weight problem, but on a personal level it seemed to be working out, so when he gave up on the course he offered me a job as his PA.

'He isn't the easiest person in the world to work for, but it made a change. In spite of everything, I'm worried about him. Why? Because I'm an idiot, I guess. Besides, it's my bread and butter and I like the work.

'The downside if you are in any way involved with Jay is that you need to have your bags packed, runway-ready, at all times, and I guess that for once mine were in the closet. The result? He did what you might call a moonlight flit on me.'

'How did you get to hear where he'd gone to?' asked Monsieur Pamplemousse.

'They telephoned from the travel agency to make sure his tickets had arrived. It was the first I knew of it, and by then it was too late. He'd gone. And that's another thing. He must have done the booking himself. My theory is he'd been keeping your Director's offer in reserve and only made up his mind at the very last moment.'

And another thing, thought Monsieur Pamplemousse; reading between the lines, it sounded very much as though Corby was doing his best to give her the slip at the same time.

Reaching a roundabout, he took a half right, heading towards the Place Louis-Armand and the train station. The sooner he found a safe hiding place for his car and an out of the way restaurant where they could eat, the better.

'This is yours?' said Amber when he stopped by his *Deux Chevaux*. 'It must be as old as Deauville itself.'

'Hardly,' said Monsieur Pamplemousse. 'But it was equally ahead of its time.'

'If it had turrets,' said Amber, 'it would go with the architecture. It looks like a roll-top desk on wheels, or a tiny tank.'

'Looks had a low priority when it was conceived,' said Monsieur Pamplemousse. 'It was designed with French farmers in view. The criterion being it should be able to travel over a freshly ploughed field at reasonable speed with a basket of fresh eggs on the back seat without breaking a single one. Which is more than you can say for a lot of today's cars. They would have a backseat full of scrambled eggs as soon as they hit the first furrow.'

'I don't know how I've managed to get through life without one,' said Amber.

'Monsieur André Citroën had his priorities right,' said Monsieur Pamplemousse.

'Talking of which . . .' feeling under the front seat he produced a copy of *Le Guide*. 'Before we go any further we must find somewhere to eat and have a good think.'

Amber reached into her bag and held up an Enprint. 'If it's of any help, I have a head and shoulders of Jay.'

Monsieur Pamplemousse took it from her and looked at it dubiously. 'At least it's bigger than mine.'

'Jay's the only person I know who's pleased with his passport photograph,' said Amber. 'This is a copy of it he had blown up. It was in a frame on his desk. Something made me bring it along just in case.'

'He doesn't look very prepossessing.'

'Nobody, but nobody except Jay, thinks their passport pic does them any favours.'

'That's because immigration people are on the lookout for other things,' said Monsieur Pamplemousse. 'The size of the ears . . . the distance between the eyes . . . the shape of the head; all these things come under the heading of Recognition Factors.'

'It's a wonder they let him through in that case,' said Amber. 'Mind you, the other nine tenths of him isn't anywhere near as bad: Reeboks, blue slacks, black button-down open collar shirt; topped by a blazer when there's a chill in the air.'

'It sounds like the same clothes he was wearing on his last visit to Paris,' said Monsieur Pamplemousse.

'It's his "Take me as you see me. Any questions?" uniform.'

'Not hard to spot in a crowd,' said Monsieur

Pamplemousse.

'It depends where you are. It hasn't been any help so far. I tried the railroad station on the way in and drew a total blank, and the staff in the Tourist Centre across the way swore he hadn't been in there either.'

'Perhaps he got the travel agency to pre-book him in somewhere . . .' suggested Monsieur Pamplemousse.

'I tried phoning them,' said Amber. 'Nothing doing. The only thing I learnt was he has an open-ended return air ticket.'

Monsieur Pamplemousse looked at her with new respect. She certainly hadn't wasted any time. He ran his finger down the list of hotels in *Le Guide.* 'The three major ones are all part of the same group. If I show the photo to the concierge at any one of them he will be able to get it scanned and circulated to the other two. It will be a start.'

'But will he bother?' She sounded doubtful.

'If I ask him nicely he will,' said Monsieur Pamplemousse. 'Besides, I know the group from my days in the Paris *Sûreté* and they're very hot on security.'

'You were in the *Sûreté?*'

'*Was* is the operative word,' said Monsieur Pamplemousse, 'although I have to admit there are times since I joined *Le Guide* when it feels as though I never left.'

He glanced at her bag. 'While we are at it, perhaps I'd better relieve you of my bottom drawer. I would hate you to be accused of shop lifting.'

Stowing the collection under the front seat alongside his guidebook, Monsieur Pamplemousse made sure they were safe from any prying eyes, then went round to the back of the car and opened the boot.

Amber looked suitably impressed when he unlocked *Le Guide*'s case to replace the binoculars.

'Very James Bond,' she said, peering over his shoulder.

'Everything from a Personal Direction Finder to a gadget for getting stones out of horses' hooves,' said Monsieur Pamplemousse. 'I have never had cause to use either, but you never know. There is always a first time.'

'I guess you might meet up with a lame horse that's lost its way,' said Amber.

Removing the top tray, Monsieur Pamplemousse found what he had been looking for.

'As for this . . .' he held up a black notebook. 'This is worth its weight in gold. There are three kinds of chef in France. Those at the top of their profession, holders of three Stock Pots and in command of a kitchen often larger than the dining area and more staff than there are patrons. Then there is the kind of chef who works wonders in an area the size of a cupboard.

'This book homes in on an area somewhere

in between. It contains a list my colleagues and I have compiled over the years of all the places we have come across on our travels that deserve to be in *Le Guide*, but for one reason or another don't want to be.'

'It sounds like a publisher's dream,' said Amber.

'And that's the way it will remain,' said Monsieur Pamplemousse. 'It would break faith with all those mentioned if their names were made public. Most of them haven't replied to any of the annual questionnaires they have been sent. Why? Because they are not interested in fame and fortune. They are perfectly happy with the way things are, thank you very much.

'*Par exemple . . .*' he flipped through the pages. 'Here is one of my own contributions. It is a little place in the Midi, not far from Orange, run by a retired bank manager, his wife and their pet dog. The Monsieur is blissfully happy tending his garden, his wife is a natural-born cook, and their dog, Ambrose, watches over it all, lending a helping paw whenever it is needed. The occasional guest provides them with the icing on the cake.'

'It sounds idyllic,' said Amber.

'In its simple way it bears comparison with Paul Bocuse, not so many kilometres away. Both are run by perfectionists. Both have what is known as "the passion" and want to share it with others. Both will ensure that you leave happier than when you arrived. But one is open to all—at a price—the other to a few passers-by who are lucky enough to be in the know. Both deserve our respect.

'Now, let us see what we can find in Deauville . . .'

'When you say "we" . . .' began Amber.

'It seems to me,' said Monsieur Pamplemousse, 'that since we share the same objective, it would be sensible to pool our resources.

'I have no wish to spend the night in the car with Pommes Frites. Not only does he take up a lot of room, but he is inclined to snore. I am assuming you will also need somewhere to stay . . .

'Ah! The very thing.' He reached for his mobile. 'It is one of Bernard's recommendations and I trust his judgement. He has good taste when it comes to looking after number one.'

'Bernard?' said Amber. 'Is he the one I met when I arrived? He helped me out of the taxi and made me feel at home straight away. It's a shame about his problem.'

'Bernard has a problem?'

'Apparently his wife is out most of the time. He sounded terribly lonely.'

How can you, Bernard? thought Monsieur Pamplemousse. *Your sins will find you out. Just wait until we next meet up!*

'Where is your luggage now?' he asked.

'I have another bag checked in at the station. Your stage-door keeper got me a taxi and explained to him where to go to pick it up at the Director's house. Such a nice man. One of nature's gentlemen. He was tickled pink when I gave him €50.'

Monsieur Pamplemousse raised his eyes heavenwards. It was no wonder old Rambaud had been smiling. May he also be forgiven.

'Fingers crossed,' said Amber. 'While you are ringing around I'll go across and check it out.'

'Two rooms facing the garden,' said Monsieur Pamplemousse when she returned. '*Diner* at 19.00. They eat early in this part of the world, but it still leaves time for a bath and a freshen-up. According to Bernard's notes, Thursday is *Poulet Vallée d'Auge* day. He rates it three Stockpots. They don't come any higher.'

'I can't wait,' said Amber.

Monsieur Pamplemousse held up the photograph of Corby. 'Before we do anything else, we need to set the wheels in motion. I must get in touch with the nearest concierge. After that I must look for a cash machine.'

He hated to think what Madame Grante would say when he handed in his P39 claim for expenses. His stock of €50 notes was rapidly diminishing, and not a single receipt! He'd better not mention that one of the beneficiaries was Rambaud. They would neither of them ever hear the last of it.

For all his faults, Bernard was a good judge of ambience, and his recommendation turned out to be an old house tucked away behind a pair of massive oak doors in a quiet part of town. It couldn't have suited Monsieur Pamplemousse better. Once the doors closed behind them, they could have been in another world, safe from prying eyes.

'Now *this* is what I call storybook France,' said Amber. 'I could never pass a pair of doors like these in Paris without wondering what lay behind them.'

If the elderly couple who lived there were in any way fazed by the arrival of such a disparate trio they showed no outward signs as they emerged to greet them.

The inside of the house was no less enchanting. His bedroom, with its whitewashed stone walls, looked out onto a flower-filled garden where a hose was playing softly amongst the shrubs. By contrast, the bathroom was state-of-the-art chrome and glass; like something out of a glossy magazine. Everything he might need was there at hand.

Looking at his watch some three quarters of an hour later, refreshed and relaxed, he went out onto the landing and knocked on Amber's door. It opened almost immediately.

She was dressed in dark blue tailored slacks topped by a close-fitting dark grey knitted sweater with a Nehru style neck. Her evening bag positively reeked Avenue Montaigne.

'Mistress of the quick change,' said Monsieur Pamplemousse, ruefully aware of his own sartorial failings.

'I've had plenty of practice,' said Amber.

'Prepare yourself for a feast,' said Monsieur Pamplemousse, as he led the way down the winding staircase and a waft of the good things in store rose to greet them.

'You are in a part of the world where the locals are not simply content with three meals a day; the truly dedicated ones eat a hearty breakfast, then they happily sit down to *tripes à la mode de Caen* for their morning break. It helps keep them going until lunchtime. Halfway through lunch they pause for a Calvados as an aid to digestion.'

'It's a funny thing . . . life,' said Amber, as they took their seats at a table near the window. She gazed round the room at the ancient furniture and fittings, the lampshades, and the pictures—mostly seascapes—adorning the walls.

'Anywhere else in the world it would be considered kitsch, but here it feels exactly right. Who would have thought it? Less than hour ago I hadn't the least idea what I was going to do next, or where my next meal was coming from, and yet here we are . . .'

'I know the feeling,' said Monsieur Pamplemousse. 'You happen to be in a certain place at a certain time, then you turn a corner

110

and your whole world changes.

'That's how things were when I happened to bump into Monsieur Leclercq. Now look at me.'

'What's your guess for tonight?'

Monsieur Pamplemousse reflected that, had he been Bernard, he would have come right out with it, adding another three Stocks Pots for the company, and no doubt asking for the name of Amber's perfume, professing himself to be overcome by it and leaning forward to drink it in. But that was Bernard.

'In this part of the world,' he said, 'think apples, butter, cream and cheese; apples for cider and Calvados, cream and butter with almost everything. For cheese you have Camembert, Livarot, Neufchâtel, and not far from where we were this afternoon, Pont-l'Evêque.

'All along the coast fish abound, perhaps not as they did in days gone by when it was said you only had to lower a bucket into the sea to catch enough to last you a week, but it's still plentiful enough.

'Mont-Saint-Michel is famous for its succulent lamb that feed off the salt grass and the many plants which grow there when the tide is out. Inland, everywhere you look there are cows grazing. Pigs are also much prized; no small-holding is without at least one, and pork butchers abound with their products.'

'So you believe in the old saying,' said

Amber. 'You are what you eat?'

'In France, generally, that is true,' said Monsieur Pamplemousse, 'but in Normandy they take it one step further. They believe that when it comes to fish and meat, you are what they ate.

'Take Montagne-au-Perche, near Alençon. There the pigs feed off windfall apples, hence it is noted for its *boudin noir.* Every year, during the third week in March, there is an International Festival.'

'You are wearing your guide hat again,' said Amber. 'Now I almost wish I hadn't asked. I shan't know what to choose.'

'You won't be given a choice,' warned Monsieur Pamplemousse. 'We shall be eating what the owners are eating and if the Madame's rosy cheeks are anything to go by, there isn't much to fear. You should follow Pommes Frites' example. He takes life as it comes.'

Hearing his name mentioned, Pommes Frites looked up happily from a large bowl of suitable sustenance put out for his benefit on a place mat. Clearly, he had made friends in the kitchen already.

The first course didn't disappoint: a *sole à la dieppoise*—its rich wine and cream sauce garnished with mussels, mushrooms and crayfish. It was accompanied by a jug of cider, with instructions to have as much of it as they liked; there was plenty more where that came

112

from.

'Home-made,' whispered Monsieur Pamplemousse.

'How do you know?' asked Amber.

Monsieur Pamplemousse filled her glass. 'It is cloudy—always a good sign. It shows it hasn't been filtered.'

'That's allowed?'

'I wouldn't like to be the person who tried to stop it. Calvados is another matter. That has to obey the same rules and regulations as Cognac.

'So what is your story?' he asked, after a moment or two had elapsed.

'I started out as a dancer,' said Amber. 'I had my eyes fixed on the ballet, but my background was against me. In England, at that time anyway, there weren't many coloured girls at Covent Garden, so I moved to France. In those days most of the top chorus lines had their quota of English girls. It was a height thing as much as anything. They all had pet names, and some of them were keen on calling me after a breakfast cereal called Special K, because it contains less than 2% fat, but I opted for Amber and for a while I never looked back.'

'What was it before?'

'Would you believe Du'aine?'

'Du'aine.' Monsieur Pamplemousse savoured it. 'Which do you prefer?'

The girl gave a shrug. 'I guess I'm used to

Amber, although after they told me at the Crazy Horse I had to go I nearly changed it to Egress.

'To fill in I had a spell in the food business. One of the barmen put me in touch with Pierre Gagnaire. Then I had a spell with Ducasse.'

'There is nothing like diving in at the deep end.'

'It was a steep learning curve,' said Amber. 'But it looks good on my CV. I learnt a lot from both of them and I'm very grateful, but waiting at tables wasn't my scene. Looks don't always help—especially if you're female. Too many men think they are God's gift and won't take "No" for an answer.

'Besides, I still wanted to dance. So I set sail for America—land of the free. At least in New York chorus lines they don't treat you as a failed ballerina. Very much the reverse.'

She sat back as the next course arrived.

'Bernard's recommendation,' said Monsieur Pamplemousse, when they were on their own again. '*Poulet Vallée d'Auge.* It combines all the typically good things about Norman cuisine in the way of local produce: apples, cider, butter, crème fraiche, mushrooms. Gastronomically, the area we are in now—the Pays d'Auge—is the richest in the whole of Normandy. This bird itself is as plump as they come.

'The crème fraiche will be from Isigny-sur-Mer. Why there in particular? Because it is the only one in all France to be awarded AOC

114

status. Crème fraiche is important to Norman recipes because it is produced naturally and it doesn't curdle when used in cooking, because despite current regulations about having to use pasteurised milk in the making, they have managed to preserve its original flavour by introducing a small amount of lactic ferment at a later stage.

'Forgive me.' He broke off. 'I am getting caught up in the technicalities again. With your background, and now working for Corby, you probably know these things already.'

Amber stared at him. 'You must be joking.'

'It stands to reason some of it must have brushed off on you.'

'Dream on,' said Amber. 'With Jay you are on your own. His method of working when he goes into a restaurant is to announce why he is there, followed by, "Better make it good—or else!"'

'With *Le Guide*,' said Monsieur Pamplemousse, 'that would be equivalent to signing our own death warrant. Anonymity is one of our key words.'

'I doubt if Jay knows the meaning of the word,' said Amber.

'But what about his books? Aren't they on the bestseller lists?'

'By chance Jay discovered he had a talent for writing the kind of things people like to read. In short, he perfected the art of digging up the dirt and cloaking it in the respectability of a guide to restaurants. It's a sad fact, but it is a rich seam. The vast mass of people would much rather read about the bad things in life than the good. Having discovered that basic fact, he never looked back.

'He leavens his reviews with a few good ones, of course, but he doesn't write those himself. That's another reason how I got to work for him. Jay knows as much about food as my Auntie Zoë did, and she was a born-again vegan who stayed that way until the day she died.

'I bet Pommes Frites knows more about gastronomy. All Jay knows is a good steak when he sees one. He likes nothing better than Sparks Steakhouse on 46th street, between 2nd and 3rd. He goes there so often he even gets a smile out of the waiters, which is saying something.'

'You don't approve?'

'I have nothing whatsoever against Sparks. If you want a great prime sirloin that's the place to go. It's well hung, for a start. *And* they have one of the best wine lists in New York. Not that that means anything to Jay. He sticks to Coca Cola.'

Monsieur Pamplemousse remembered the glass Corby had been clutching at the party.

'They're good on quality control,' he admitted. 'It's the one drink you can guarantee will be the same anywhere in the world. I'm amazed the Director had it in stock.'

'Jay would have brought his own. He doesn't take any chances. He even carries his own swizzlestick.'

'Swizzlestick?' repeated Monsieur Pamplemousse.

'Swizzle is an old English term for mixing alcoholic drinks,' said Amber. 'Don't ask me why. A swizzlestick is what you use to make them froth up. You can also use it to get rid of the bubbles in champagne and Coca Cola.'

'The first sounds like sacrilege,' said Monsieur Pamplemousse. 'I have no views about the second.'

'Jay swears by its medicinal properties. It's supposed to cure major dehydration, but to take full advantage of it you have to remove the carbon dioxide. End of lesson.'

Monsieur Pamplemousse gazed at her curiously. 'So what is his problem?'

'He is like a lot of present-day food critics. He uses his column to air his views about anything other than food. In his case, there is also a sadistic streak at work. He likes nothing better than to find a restaurant he can really get his teeth into and do a hatchet job on it. Unfortunately, he did it once too often.

'What your boss fails to realise is that he only agreed to his invitation at the last minute because he saw it as a means of going into hiding.'

Looking round to make certain the Madame was nowhere around and they couldn't be overheard, Amber lowered her voice.

'He gave such a bad review to a restaurant it had to close down.'

'There's nothing new in that, surely?' said Monsieur Pamplemousse. 'It happens from time to time.'

'This one was in Las Vegas,' said Amber. 'And it happened to be Mafia territory. It was home from home to some of the big names in the local family.'

'Surely whoever it belonged to, they won't follow him over here?'

'Don't you believe it. You don't do that kind of thing with the Mafia and get away with it. Word has gone out. Currently, Jay is trying to put clear water between him and the Mob and that won't be easy. They have long arms and even longer memories.'

The clearing of the table and the arrival of a large bowl interrupted her story.

'*Teurgoule*,' said Monsieur Pamplemousse briefly.

'It looks like rice pudding to me,' whispered Amber.

'But made with cream and flavoured with cinnamon,' said Monsieur Pamplemousse. 'The brioche that comes with it is a local delicacy. It's a mixture of syrup and yeast.'

'Do you think the Madame will be very upset if I don't have any?' asked Amber.

'Mortified,' said Monsieur Pamplemousse. 'But I daresay Pommes Frites will help out if you ask him nicely.'

'So what happened?' he asked, when order had been restored.

'What happened was . . .' continued Amber, 'I had been away from the office for a couple of days, and when I arrived back I smelt emptiness the moment I opened the door. You know how it is . . .'

'There is a difference between someone being out of a room and their having gone for good,' said Monsieur Pamplemousse.

'Exactly! On Jay's desk there was an unopened box. It was supposedly from some gourmet meat suppliers, but I guess it had been made up specially. It was labelled in big letters: FOR THE MAN WHO HAS EVERYTHING. The s on "HAS" had been crossed out and a D inserted.

'Inside the plastic window in the top of the box you could see various goodies, like a heart, liver and other odd bits and pieces, including what looked like a bull's ding dong and its associated items, which had already been detached.

'Alongside the box, attached to a bloodstained Japanese degutting knife, was a hand-written note in block letters saying "ANY DAY NOW ALL THIS COULD BE YOURS".

'Surprise, surprise! There was no sign of Jay.

'He'd been sitting on your director's invitation for quite a while, holding out for more money, I guess. The latest happening

119

made up his mind for him on the spot.'

Monsieur Pamplemousse couldn't help thinking the Director must have been holding his breath too. It was no wonder he had been a bit cagey.

'In case you didn't notice, everything at your party was OK until the press moved in after the show and one of them started trying to take pictures of Jay. That's why he went bananas. He would have seen it as a dead giveaway, with the accent on *dead*. Had any of the pictures hit the front page, as well they might given his penchant for publicity and the fact that it's the flat season news-wise, the Mafia would be on to him like a shot.

'Jay isn't a great one for heroics at the best of times. He's like a lot of bullies. Underneath it all he wouldn't be capable of setting a mouse trap in case the mouse turned on him.'

'All that being so,' said Monsieur Pamplemousse thoughtfully, 'this isn't necessarily the best place to be. Wherever there is a casino, crime isn't far away, and Deauville is probably no exception. It acts like a magnet. Given that it also has two race-courses . . .'

'So you think he may move on?'

'If he has any sense he will.'

'What are the options?'

'If his aim is to disappear, his best bet would be to lie low in a city, the bigger the better. Any departure from the norm in the country stands out like a sore thumb and is a matter for comment. City people are mostly only interested in themselves and their immediate surroundings.'

'Any suggestions on that score?' asked Amber. 'I mean, what would be the best route out?'

'In theory,' said Monsieur Pamplemousse, 'he has a wide choice: by land, sea or air. On land, he could hire a car . . .'

'Jay can't drive.'

'In that case there is a bus service linking Deauville with Caen and Le Havre . . .'

Amber looked dubious. 'Somehow I can't picture it.'

'Another possibility would be to take a taxi. But taxi drivers have a habit of talking amongst themselves . . .

'As for the sea, there are plenty of private yachts in the harbour . . . but I have no idea if there is anything larger. We could check in the morning. I daresay it wouldn't be difficult to hire a boat to take him along the coast. It would be less conspicuous than any other way.'

'How about flying?'

'There is an airport at St-Gatien-des-Bois, eight kilometers out of Deauville, but it is comparatively small and seasonal. Again, as far as I recall it caters mostly for the extremely well-heeled: charter planes, helicopters, high-level poker players, millionaires flying in from places like Marrakech and Athens for the yearling horse sales in August, that kind of thing.

'The downside is that almost certainly the paparazzi will be hanging around on the lookout for familiar faces. It will be ten times worse in a few weeks' time when *La Saison* is in full swing and the boardwalk becomes a catwalk.

'In short, it is nowhere near as easy as it might sound. To get somewhere major he would need to a take a train inland as far as Lisieux and pick up an express to wherever. At this time of night I doubt if there is much choice, if any.'

'So you think it would be safe to leave things until the morning?'

'That would be my instinct.'

Amber eyed her empty plate. 'That was a delicious meal. Everything you said it would be. But I can't eat another thing.'

'No cheese?' asked Monsieur Pamplemousse. 'I'm sure Madame has a wonderful selection . . .'

Amber gave a mock shudder. 'No cheese, nothing . . .'

'Brillat-Savarin once said, "A dessert without cheese is like a beautiful woman with only one eye."'

'Well, Brillat-Savarin probably hadn't travelled overnight from New York,' said Amber. 'And both my eyes are telling me it's time for bed.'

Monsieur Pamplemousse had to confess he was feeling much the same way. It could be the sea air. 'But first,' he said, looking down at the recumbent figure on the floor, 'certain of us are probably in need of a constitutional.'

Goodnights exchanged, and having tendered their apologies to the Madame, he set out shortly afterwards with Pommes Frites.

Both were lost in thought. Pommes Frites was still wondering where he had gone wrong with his master's present, and Monsieur Pamplemousse was turning over in his mind the ramifications behind the news about Corby. There was still one card he could play.

A turn around the block sufficed for both of them. The streets were empty. The lights from the seafront and the casino, just a glow in the sky. Amber was right. It was time for bed.

On their return, they were creeping as quietly as possible back to his room when her door opened. She was wearing a silk nightdress of such minute proportions it did rather less than nothing to hide her figure, and once again he was aware of her perfume.

'I have been thinking,' said Amber. 'I take your point about being better off in a city rather than somewhere in the country, but seeing this is the holiday season, wouldn't Jay do just as well sticking to this part of the world for the time being? I don't mean here in Deauville necessarily. That's a bit too obvious. But somewhere else that attracts the crowds.'

'You could be right,' said Monsieur Pamplemousse.

'May I claim my reward?' said Amber.

Compared with the moment in the changing room her goodnight kiss was somewhere off the top of the Richter scale. Pommes Frites' tail went rigid on his master's behalf.

'I have also been thinking,' said Monsieur Pamplemousse, when he came back down to earth. 'Were you with Ducasse when he threw that enormous party in Versailles to celebrate Paul Bocuse's eightieth birthday? Over three hundred guests.'

Amber shook her head. 'It was a little before my time.'

'Pity. It must have been a mammoth task for one chef.'

'That's Ducasse for you. They still talked about it when I was there.'

Monsieur Pamplemousse couldn't help but notice the bed in the background. A *grand lit*, no less, its cover turned invitingly back.

'It is very large for one person,' said Amber, following his eyes. 'Large but lonely.'

'Sometimes,' said Monsieur Pamplemousse, 'a bed can be the loneliest place in the world. Besides, two's company and three's a crowd. Pommes Frites is probably tired out after his performance and he can be a dead weight at the best of times.'

'His right leg must be nearly falling off,' said Amber. 'I've heard some excuses in my time.'

Monsieur Pamplemousse also had some telephone calls to make, but he kept that fact to himself.

'Is everything all right, Aristide?' asked Doucette when she answered his call. 'Your voice sounds funny.'

'It is probably the sea air, Couscous,' he said.

Before he went to sleep, Monsieur Pamplemousse made one more call. This time it was to enquire after Monsieur Leclercq's health. He rather hoped the Director wouldn't pick up the phone himself. He was in no mood to cope with what could be a long and tedious explanation.

The distaff side came to his rescue.

'The local *pompiers* managed to release him,' said Chantal. 'They had to make use of a scenery hoist. He is now in a darkened room nursing his wounds. One of our English guests suggested he might need counselling. An American friend came up with the idea of an Anger Management course. You can imagine how both of those went down. I think they are now the ones who are in need of help.'

Monsieur Pamplemousse gave her a brief rundown on Corby's problem before getting down to brass tacks.

'Talking of the Mafia,' he said. 'Have you heard from your Sicilian uncle recently?'

'Uncle Caputo? Not since he intervened when Henri was being blackmailed and you and Pommes Frites became involved.'

'He may be able to help again,' said Monsieur Pamplemousse. 'Given Deauville has both a casino and two race tracks, it is possible he has contacts in this part of the world. As you may remember, following on from the last affair, he gained himself a new driver . . . a remarkably good one, so he owes me a favour.'

'Two favours if you count the girl who tried to seduce Henri on the flight back from New York,' said Chantal. 'Maria was her name, I think. I gather she has also been taken on strength.'

'You know about her?' said Monsieur Pamplemousse.

'I do now,' said Chantal. 'I always suspected as much, but thank you for confirming it.

'Henri doesn't know I know,' she added.

'I promise not to tell him,' said Monsieur Pamplemousse.

'It is better that way,' said Chantal. 'There is no fool like an old fool and despite everything I do love him very much.'

'So . . .'

'I will do my best, Aristide. I cannot do more. *Dormez bien.*'

Dormez bien, thought Monsieur Pamplemousse bitterly, as he turned off his light.

It's all right for some. For others, the chance would be a fine thing.

He was right about one thing, though.

Pommes Frites really was a dead weight.

CHAPTER SIX

If Friday got off to a bad start, it was for a very good reason.

As is so often the case when a person doesn't get a good night's sleep, but whiles away the time instead tossing and turning, his or her mind occupied by this, that and 'the other' (the 'other' being an especially well-documented cause of chronic insomnia), the inevitable happens, and Monsieur Pamplemousse was no exception to the rule.

Shortly before dawn, worn out by it all, he slipped gently but firmly into the welcoming arms of Morpheus. And that was where he remained for the next few hours, held in a vice-like grip, to all intents and purposes dead to the world.

So much so, Pommes Frites, having taken several close looks at his master, even went so far as to try giving him a nudge or two, but without success.

Having slept through the wake-up call from a built-in bedside alarm carefully set for 07.00, Monsieur Pamplemousse eventually woke to the insistent ringing of a telephone on the other side of the room.

It took him a moment or two to realise it

was coming from his own mobile, which he had left on charge, and longer still to recognise the voice as that of the concierge he had spoken to the previous evening.

'Apropos your enquiry, Monsieur . . .' repeated the man, relieved to have made contact at long last. 'It appears the gentleman concerned was staying at one of our associated hotels. I thought you might like to know that earlier this morning he was asking about the availability of early morning trains departing from Deauville . . .

'*Oui*, Monsieur. *Most* regrettable. My opposite number on duty during the day left a note for his colleague on the nightshift. As it happened, he didn't realise the importance of the matter until a few minutes ago when he came across the photograph you allowed me to copy, and put two and two together . . .

'I do agree, Monsieur . . . Words fail me too. I am *desolé*. But the gentleman concerned appears to be travelling under a different name . . . a Monsieur Jay . . .

'*Oui*, Monsieur. Unfortunately, the weakest link in any chain is often the hardest one to spot.

'I will certainly pass your message on to the person concerned at the earliest possible moment . . .

'*Oui*, Monsieur . . . I will tell the man he is an idiot . . .

'*Oui*, Monsieur, heads will undoubtedly roll . . .

'In the meantime, to bring matters up to date, you may be interested to know that the gentleman you were enquiring about decided to take the 09.15 a.m. train to Lisieux . . .

'He checked out about a half an hour ago and the hotel car took him to the station . . .

'No, Monsieur, he didn't say where he was heading for after that . . .'

Monsieur Pamplemousse glanced at his watch. It was past nine o'clock already . . . '*Merde!*'

'*Exactement,* Monsieur . . . Most unfortunate. If I can be of any further assistance . . .'

Terminating the call, Monsieur Pamplemousse dashed across the room—it was no time to suggest that for a start a refund of his €50 would not come amiss; the question would almost certainly have triggered off an attack of amnesia.

Rapping as hard as he could on the wall adjoining Amber's bedroom, he leapt into the air nursing his knuckles. The solid stone felt at least half a metre thick.

Hearing a second cry of '*merde*' in almost as many seconds, Pommes Frites was about to hurry across the room in order to render first aid, when his master went into overdrive. Following a brief conversation on the house telephone, both bathroom taps were turned fully on, cupboard doors flung open . . .

Since all the signs pointed to a hasty departure, Pommes Frites sought shelter for the time being behind the far side of the bed in order to carry out his own ablutions in peace, whilst at same time keeping a low profile and watching points.

Following Monsieur Pamplemousse into the corridor some fifteen or so minutes later, he couldn't help but notice the girl, who had been waiting outside their room with her bag already packed, bend down to adjust one of his master's trouser legs, the end of which had become caught in a sock.

It was a task normally carried out most mornings when they were at home by Madame Pamplemousse, and there was no reason in the world why someone else shouldn't do it. It was simply a matter of territories, an uninvited crossing of boundaries, so without making a song and dance about it, Pommes Frites kept his counsel, storing the information away for future reference.

He doubted if his master had even noticed. His mind was clearly on other things.

Once again it was a case of abject apologies being tendered to their hosts.

The first time it had been for leaving the evening meal unfinished; clearly an event beyond the realms of their understanding. Now came the even harder task of explaining their hasty departure rather than linger over a sumptuous breakfast laid out for their benefit on a table in the garden.

If the couple were at all put out by the array of *patisseries*, *confiture* and bowls of fruit going begging, they hid their feelings remarkably well, which was more than could be said for the ubiquitous sparrows hovering overhead; possibly the same ones that frequented the beach later in the day. Scarcely believing their good fortune, saliva all but dripped from their beaks.

With calls of *'bonne journée'* still echoing round the courtyard, Monsieur Pamplemousse waited for the huge doors to swing shut behind them, then, following the signposts, made for the D677 heading inland to Pont-l'Evéque and beyond.

'It's a terrible shame,' said Amber.

'C'est la vie.' Monsieur Pamplemousse shrugged his shoulders, concentrating on the drive ahead.

'Do you think we shall make it?'

He glanced at his watch, then gave a groan as a garbage truck came to a halt in front of them, effectively blocking the narrow road. 'At this rate we certainly won't catch up with the train. Lisieux is only twenty minutes away by rail. It all depends on what connection Corby is aiming for once he gets there.'

Taking a hand off the steering wheel, he felt in his jacket pocket for a timetable he had picked up as a matter of course while getting

Doucette's ticket. Attempting to pass it over his shoulder as they rounded a bend, it cascaded open, enveloping Pommes Frites' head.

'Does he usually travel in the front seat?' asked Amber, carefully unwinding the concertina-like folds.

'It happens to have the only safety belt in the car that fits him,' said Monsieur Pamplemousse simply. 'The last thing we need is to be stopped by the police before we hit the open road. Besides, he acts as a stabiliser. As you have no doubt noticed, he is a great help going round bends at speed. There are occasions when I don't know what I would do without him.'

'And there are some things I would rather not know!' said Amber.

'Perhaps you can find what trains the 09.15 might connect with,' suggested Monsieur Pamplemousse.

Amber was silent for several minutes. 'I'm glad I don't work in a booking office,' she said at last. 'It's no wonder they always have such long queues. All of them seem to have a different number tacked on. From number 1: "Every day except *sam, dim et fêtes*", to number 34, which simply says: "*le 11 nov.*"'

'In this part of the world,' said Monsieur Pamplemousse, 'that undoubtedly refers to an Armistice Day special for people visiting the D-Day landing beaches. I can't help with the others.'

'As far as I can tell,' said Amber, 'and don't quote me in case I'm wrong, but there should be a semi-fast train to Paris leaving at 10.05.'

'If he's aiming for that,' said Monsieur Pamplemousse gloomily, 'we're sunk. Our only hope is that it may have been delayed for some reason.'

*   *   *

Pont l'Evêque came and went, and it was 10.08 by the time they arrived outside Lisieux Station. Parking haphazardly in the first available space, Monsieur Pamplemousse led the rush inside.

But it was a wasted effort. The vast expanse of tarmac separating the arrival and the departure areas was deserted, as indeed were the *quais* themselves.

Seeing the look of disappointment on his master's face and realising some kind of disaster had taken place, Pommes Frites let out a spectacular howl. Normally it would have been a conversation-stopper, but it produced quite the opposite effect.

Had an unannounced high-speed TGV roared through the station without stopping, it could hardly have been more effective. Uniformed figures appeared as if by magic from all directions.

At their head was the *Chef de Gare*, a

magisterial figure with a waxed moustache and a clipboard, who had clearly drummed it into his subordinates that their main role in life was to shepherd flocks of idiot passengers across the wide expanse between the two *quais* in case they got lost en route while changing trains.

Summing up the situation at a glance, he dismissed the rest of the staff in order that he might deal effectively with the new arrivals.

It seemed that Corby had indeed caught the 10.05 to Paris, scheduled to arrive there at 11.46.

He pointed to a lamp standard further along the platform. 'That is the very spot where the first class carriage stops. I helped him board the train myself. He seemed confused, almost as though he didn't really want to get on it. His mind was clearly elsewhere.

'Prior to that, he was making enquiries about trains to Alsace-Lorraine. I advised him that when he reaches Paris he takes a taxi to the Gare de l'Est and boards a TGV. He should be in plenty of time for the 12.24, which arrives in Strasbourg at 14.43.

'The next train to Paris, Monsieur? There is one at 10.49.'

'Just in time to miss the 12.24 to Strasbourg, I presume?' said Monsieur Pamplemousse.

'It allows ample time to miss the 12.24 to Strasbourg, Monsieur,' said the *Chef de Gare* dryly. 'I am afraid it is a stopping train. It doesn't arrive in Paris until 13.36, but there is a refreshment service on board.'

Monsieur Pamplemousse and Amber exchanged glances.

'I'm starving,' said Amber. 'It was the sight of that breakfast going begging this morning as they waved us goodbye.'

'First things first,' said Monsieur Pamplemousse. Reaching for his mobile he pointed to a nearby bench. 'I must telephone the Director.'

'*Donner und Blitzen!*' said Amber, as she sat down beside him.

Monsieur Pamplemousse eyed her curiously. 'Why do you say that?'

'What?'

'*Donner und Blitzen.*'

'Because I can hear Jay saying it. He uses it a lot. Half jokingly, of course . . . it sort of figures, seeing he was born in that part of the world.'

'You think he might be making for home?'

'With Jay, these things depend very much on whether you are buying or selling, but most of the time two and two make four.'

Monsieur Pamplemousse dialled the Leclercqs' number.

The Director's wife picked up on the second ring. It sounded as though she had been expecting his call.

'Bad news all round, I'm afraid.

'I spoke to Uncle Caputo after you phoned

135

last night. He sends his regards, but said he was sorry he couldn't interfere. I quote: "If this guy gave one of my restaurants a bad review, you think I would shake him by the hand?" I am sorry, Aristide, but . . .'

'I understand,' said Monsieur Pamplemousse. 'It *is* very disappointing, of course. However, I appreciate that in his situation the family must come first . . .

'And Monsieur? How is he today?'

'He is getting better, I'm afraid,' said Chantal. 'He is like a cat on hot bricks. Have you seen today's journals?'

'I haven't even had breakfast yet,' admitted Monsieur Pamplemousse.

'Ah! Well, in that case before you speak to Henri, I recommend you have a small black coffee and a large Calvados standing by.'

'I'm afraid neither is possible at this moment,' said Monsieur Pamplemousse. 'If you like, I could ring back . . .'

But his words were wasted. The longish silence that followed was interspersed with the sound of rustling paper, during which Monsieur Pamplemousse heard his name being mentioned more than once.

'Have you seen today's journals, Pamplemousse?' boomed Monsieur Leclercq, echoing his wife's words when he at last came on the phone. 'Have you seen them?'

'No, Monsieur,' said Monsieur Pamplemousse patiently. 'As I was telling

Madame Leclercq, I haven't even had breakfast.' He nearly said 'we' but stopped himself just in time.

'Just listen to this then . . .'

'One moment, Monsieur.' Monsieur Pamplemousse beckoned Amber nearer.

'SEX ON THE SANDS . . .' The Director's voice came through loud and clear.

'PANIC ON LA PLANCHE . . . DOG-TOTING VAMPIRE STRIKES AT VERY HEART OF DEAUVILLE.

'Deauville of all places, Aristide. In all the years Chantal and I have been coming here nothing like it has ever happened before. I am at a loss for words.'

Monsieur Pamplemousse felt tempted to point out that it was more than could be said of the headline writers. To put it mildly, they had well and truly gone to town. But something in the Director's voice, a certain hesitation, put him off the idea.

'Tell me, Aristide,' said Monsieur Leclercq, 'I take it you are using your mobile.'

'*Oui*, Monsieur.'

'Is it a new one?'

'No, Monsieur. It is the same old one. I find the latest models far from my liking. For a start they are much too light. Try making a film with one of them and it is like watching someone using a hosepipe to spray their roses.'

'How very strange,' said the Director. 'It sounds for all the world as though it has built-in translation facilities. One gets used to the many things one can use them for these days, but I have never come across that before. It is an interesting development, Aristide; one we might make use of as part of our basic equipment for those on the road.'

Monsieur Pamplemousse wondered whether he should let the Director know he was simply providing Amber with an English version of the headlines before the worst happened and he got carried away by issuing a bulk order. He decided against it. Explanations would be tedious beyond belief.

'I was merely practising my English, Monsieur,' he said, clutching at straws. 'I may need it when we catch up with Corby.'

'Positive thinking, Pamplemousse,' said the Director. 'That is what I like to hear. There are times when I don't know what I would do without you.

'CANINE CAPERS HIT NEW LOW,' he continued. Having got the bit between his teeth there was no stopping him.

'It appears there is a hound of extraordinarily vast proportions involved. By all accounts it is somewhat reminiscent of the Hound of the Baskervilles, only much bigger. Apparently it mesmerises everyone it comes into contact with. There is a graphic description given by a child in one of the journals.'

Monsieur Pamplemousse waited while there

was yet another rustling of paper.

'*Anita Duval-Marchant (5), described in no uncertain terms her narrow escape. "I felt its hot breath all over my dinner," she said. "I didn't dare touch the plate afterwards. I shall never, ever, eat spinach again. It has put me off it for life!"*'

'A typical journalese flight of fancy,' broke in Monsieur Pamplemousse, unable to contain himself a moment longer. 'They should check their facts. The nearest Pommes Frites got to her was when he returned from a dip in the ocean. While shaking himself dry, he happened to splash her. Besides, she didn't like spinach in the first place.'

'Pommes Frites?' repeated Monsieur Leclercq. 'Where were you last night, Pamplemousse, may I ask? Perhaps your recent response to my questionnaire was not so wide of the mark after all.'

'We spent the evening with a friend,' said Monsieur Pamplemousse virtuously. 'We had *Poulet Vallée d'Auge*—'

'Made with cider and crème fraîche from Isigny-sur-Mer?'

'Of course, Monsieur.'

'Ah, how I envy you, Aristide. After my release, I was forbidden to eat a thing until I received the all-clear from a member of the medical profession and by then it was too late in the day.'

'He hasn't lost his sense of priorities,'

139

whispered Monsieur Pamplemousse.

'We didn't budge from our table until it was time for bed, Monsieur . . .' he continued for fear the Director might question him further, but he needn't have worried.

'It seems that not only has someone been distributing obscene pictures along the boardwalk,' said Monsieur Leclercq, 'but the local police have unearthed a cache of ladies undergarments hidden in the sand. What I believe are commonly referred to as panties in America. How they got there, and for what nefarious reason, goodness only knows. If the story reaches the other side of the Atlantic and our name becomes associated with it, *Zagat* won't let it rest. It will be yet another nail in our coffin.'

'I brought you all the ones that were there,' hissed Amber.

'Someone with malice aforethought must have topped it up,' whispered Monsieur Pamplemousse.

'They are anxious to interview anyone who can lay claim to ownership,' said Monsieur Leclercq. 'But so far no one has come forward.'

'I'm not surprised,' murmured Amber. 'I certainly wouldn't.'

'You already have,' whispered Monsieur Pamplemousse. 'Remember?'

'What was that?' barked the Director. 'It sounds as though there is someone else on the line. I keep hearing extraneous voices.'

Monsieur Pamplemousse covered the mouthpiece as best he could and suppressed a sigh.

'I'm sorry about this.'

'Normally,' said Monsieur Leclercq, 'I would have hazarded a guess that these things, occurring in quick succession as they have, bear all the hallmarks of past escapades, Pamplemousse.

'However, the police have issued a description of the man they are looking for. It is only an artist's impression, of course, based on information gleaned from questioning on-the-spot witnesses, but fortunately it leaves you totally in the clear. The person they are seeking looks remarkably like a cross between Clark Gable and Errol Flynn.

'I know comparisons are odious, Aristide, but the thought of your being mistaken for either one of them is quite laughable; an amalgam of the two beggars belief.'

Monsieur Pamplemousse was rapidly revising his opinion of women's ability to remember faces.

'The truth is, Monsieur,' he said stiffly, 'people often see what they want to see. It is a well-known fact that beauty is in the eye of the beholder. Over and above that, there are many ladies who prefer an older, more mature man.'

'Not *that* old, Pamplemousse, surely?'

'It takes all sorts,' said Monsieur

141

Pamplemousse. 'Each to his or her own. On the other side of the coin, I am told there are those who, when they reach a certain age, hanker after the thought of an urgent young body lying beside them. In their mind's eye they picture their dream man arriving on a white horse and, as the sun sets on the distant horizon, riding off with them lashed to the pommel of his saddle.'

'Well, that certainly lets you out, Pamplemousse,' said Monsieur Leclercq. 'You would only have to turn up in your *Deux Chevaux* and such ideas would go flying out through the bedroom window, especially if the passenger door came off its hinges and fell into the gutter, as I am told happened on one occasion. You would need to make certain they were tightly lashed to the bonnet in case that fell off too!'

'At least it would keep them warm,' said Monsieur Pamplemousse.

The Director ignored the interruption. 'Just think, Aristide,' he mused. 'Had things been different there might have been a hut on the boardwalk bearing your name.'

Monsieur Pamplemousse put his hand over the mouthpiece. 'He seems to have forgotten all about the matter in hand.'

'All of which,' boomed Monsieur Leclercq, 'leads me to the matter in hand. The things I have mentioned would be completely beside the point were it not for the fact that they are all too unusual to be simply coincidental. They must be tied in with Corby in some way.

'Chantal has brought me up to date with all you told her last night and if the Mafia are involved it puts an entirely different complexion on the matter. Who knows what machinations are going on beneath the surface? The Mob will stop at nothing. It is no wonder he fears for his life.'

'From *Le Guide*'s point of view,' said Monsieur Pamplemousse, 'it does mean that almost certainly he won't be catching the next plane back to America. Also, if he is on the run, giving us a bad write-up will be the last thing on his mind. On the other hand, he won't be giving us a good one either . . . With a little bit of luck it could be the last we shall hear of him.'

'And the whole exercise will have been a wasted effort,' broke in the Director. 'That is what grieves me most, Aristide. It as an old saying of Pasteur's, but a very true one: "Luck smiles on minds that are prepared". I rather fear, Pamplemousse, that for whatever reason, your own mind would appear to be elsewhere at present.

'If the worst comes to pass and the Mafia catch up with Corby, the press will have a field day with what is left of him. The reason for his being in France in the first place will make headline news all over the world. What is the name of that American press photographer who is notorious for always being on the spot when mayhem occurs? I remember seeing an exhibition of his pictures in Paris. Squeegie something or other?'

'WeeGee,' said Monsieur Pamplemousse. 'He is no longer with us, I fear, and when he was alive, more often than not he enjoyed the benefit of rather more inside information than I possess.'

'Be that as it may, Aristide, we must stay with it for the time being. I shall not rest easy in my bed until we know what has happened to Corby.'

'There is a distinct possibility,' said Monsieur Pamplemousse, baiting the hook, 'that he may be returning to a part of France where he was born . . . Alsace-Lorraine.'

'Then you must go after him, Pamplemousse,' said the Director. 'No matter what the cost, no stone must be left unturned . . .'

Monsieur Pamplemousse felt a nudge. He had no need to look round.

'There is one slight problem, Monsieur . . . The person I was dining with yesterday evening happens to be Monsieur Corby's general factotum. You may not be aware of the fact, but she arrived not long before we left for the theatre. She is as worried as anyone about what has happened to him. Indeed, it is she who suggested that may be where he is heading for at this very moment.'

'Excellent news, Pamplemousse,' broke in Monsieur Leclercq. 'She will be *une bonne accessoire* in your hunt. Women have an eye for detail.'

'You did say whatever the cost,' ventured Monsieur Pamplemousse. 'I am thinking of Madame Grante . . .'

'I will take care of Madame Grante,' broke in the Director sternly. 'This is no occasion for her cheeseparing ways.'

'In that case,' said Monsieur Pamplemousse, 'there is also the small matter of my car. It is parked outside the *gare* in Lisieux.'

'Leave it to me, Aristide,' said Monsieur Leclercq grandly. 'Have no fear, I shall make all the necessary arrangements.'

'I will leave the keys in the exhaust pipe,' said Monsieur Pamplemousse.

'So?' Amber looked at him expectantly as he terminated the call.

'He said you would be a useful adjunct.'

'I've been called a lot of things in my life,' said Amber. 'But an adjunct . . .'

'All expenses paid.'

'That's different. It definitely has a nice ring to it.'

'I have no wish to dampen your spirits,' said Monsieur Pamplemousse, leading the way towards the ticket office, 'but not to put too fine a point on matters, it could be a dead-end job.'

Amber made a face. 'That aside, I still can't

145

believe all the headlines in the papers.'

'They are blown up out of all proportion,' said Monsieur Pamplemousse, 'and I think I know the reason why.

'It is a classic case of attack being the best form of defence, and someone must have friends in high places. Don't forget today is Friday.'

'What difference does that make?'

'Husbands will be coming down from Paris for the weekend, their suspicions aroused. The wives are getting their side of the story in first with a vengeance.'

'Don't tell me their spouses will be coming after you as well?'

'Suitably primed,' said Monsieur Pamplemousse, 'anything is possible.'

Producing his wallet, he paid for two tickets to Paris.

'Shouldn't you have bought one for Pommes Frites?' asked Amber, as they made their way onto the platform.

'If I had done that,' said Monsieur Pamplemousse, 'the woman who sold them to me would have wanted to see his muzzle. It is required by law for dogs above a certain size. He would have been mortified.'

The subject was hastily changed as they were waylaid by the *Chef de Gare*. He removed a slip of paper from his clipboard and handed it to Monsieur Pamplemousse. It was a printout of the TGV service between Paris and

Strasbourg.

'Do you think he's like this with everyone?' asked Amber, after they had been helped onto the train and safely seated. 'He couldn't have been more solicitous.'

'If he is,' said Monsieur Pamplemousse, 'and I rather suspect that is the case, it is no wonder Corby was twitchy. He was probably doing his best to slip onto the train unnoticed.'

Once they were on the move he excused himself and gave Doucette a quick call.

'I'm heading back to Paris.'

'How wonderful!' said Doucette.

'It isn't quite as simple as that, Couscous. I'm simply passing through on my way to Strasbourg and I thought you would like to know—'

'Don't tell me Monsieur Corby is mixed up in all the troubles I've been reading about?'

'It is in the Paris papers too?'

'Headline news! And on this morning's radio. I think a lot of the press must have stayed on after your play and picked up on it. That's not the only thing. Just you wait until you see the reviews . . .'

'It *is* the so-called silly season for news . . .' began Monsieur Pamplemousse.

Out of the corner of his eye he saw a uniformed figure approaching. 'Look, Couscous, it is not the best time to talk. I will ring again in a little while . . .'

Terminating the call, he was just in time to

cue Pommes Frites, who let out a minor growl to begin with, ending up as though relishing a particularly succulent bone.

Studiously ignoring him and having checked their tickets, the man disappeared back down the coach the way he had come.

'Is Pommes Frites trained to do that automatically?' asked Amber, looking impressed.

'Would you ask a bloodhound for his ticket?' said Monsieur Pamplemousse. 'Especially one without a muzzle. It is a simple case of *"C'est interdit! Mais toléré."*'

'It is forbidden, but it is tolerated,' repeated Amber. 'Trust you French to have a phrase for it.'

'It is less devious than the English equivalent,' said Monsieur Pamplemousse. '"What the eye doesn't see the heart doesn't grieve for."'

'Touché!' said Amber. 'Does he know any other useful tricks?'

'It was not for nothing that he won the Pierre Armand Sniffer Dog of the Year Award,' said Monsieur Pamplemousse fondly.

'Sniffing is one thing,' said Amber. 'Those growls were something else again.'

'Monsieur Armand was one of the greatest animal trainers ever known,' said Monsieur Pamplemousse. 'Nothing was beyond him.' Reaching for his wallet again he felt inside one of the compartments and produced a faded sepia photograph.

'Coincidentally, he is not unlike the stationmaster at Lisieux. Sadly, they don't make them like that any more.'

'But he only has one arm,' said Amber.

'The picture was taken soon after he first started,' said Monsieur Pamplemousse. 'He was working in a circus and he was teaching a lion to eat out of his hand. It was a salutary lesson, but from that moment on he knew where his destiny lay—'

'I think I would have known where mine lay if it had happened to me,' said Amber. 'And it wouldn't have had anything to do with the circus.'

'In Monsieur Armand's case, it acted as a spur,' said Monsieur Pamplemousse.

'So, how did you get Pommes Frites to growl?'

Monsieur Pamplemousse touched his right ear and Pommes Frites automatically obeyed the command.

'When it comes to an audible display of emotions,' he said, 'growling and barking to order is fairly easy; it's much harder teaching a dog *not* to bark when danger threatens. It goes against their natural instincts. It is second only to going off on their own assignments, yet remaining true to their handler's wishes. Pommes Frites received maximum marks in both; growling and barking when he was called upon to do so and acting with the utmost stealth of his own accord when the occasion demanded it.'

'You don't have to tell me,' said Amber. 'But what happens if you touch your left ear?'

'Stand clear everybody,' said Monsieur Pamplemousse. 'Or, as your Monsieur Corby might say, "*Donner und Blitzen*".'

'His name is Korbinian,' said Amber, taking the hint. 'His father was born in Southern Germany, near München. He married a girl from Alsace and they eventually settled near Strasbourg, which was where Jay was born. The pet form of Korbinian is Körbl, so when he first emigrated to America he decided to take the plunge and make it Corby. Eventually, he assumed it along with the first name—Jay.

'How do I know all this? For the same reason that you asked me about *Donner und Blitzen* in the first place.'

Lost in thought, Monsieur Pamplemousse gazed out of the window.

'You have gone very quiet, Aristide,' said Amber after a while. 'Is it something I said?'

'No,' said Monsieur Pamplemousse. 'Quite the reverse. It was a remark someone else made.'

'Do I get to know who it was?'

'The *Chef de Gare* at Lisieux. If you remember, he said that when he helped Corby onto the train he appeared reluctant to go, almost as though he were having second

150

thoughts.'

'It was hard to resist him,' said Amber. 'If you remember, he even waved us goodbye as the train pulled out.'

'Precisely,' said Monsieur Pamplemousse. 'If he was anything like half as solicitous as he was with us, there would have been no question of Corby *not* getting on the train. It could have been the last thing he wanted to do.

'Add to that the fact that, from knowing nothing about his plans, we suddenly have a surfeit of information, I smell a rat.'

'What do you think brought it on?'

'A garbled message perhaps. Or a simple misunderstanding. Akin to someone asking the time off another person with a digital watch and having been told it is 22.11, they go on their way happy in the belief that it is only twenty minutes to eleven and they have all the time in the world, when in fact they haven't.'

'A chain reaction gone doubly wrong?'

'*Exactement!* It might even be that the concierge at the hotel where Corby was staying told him someone had been enquiring after him.'

'That would be enough—'

'Do you still have the timetable I gave you?'

Amber flipped open the concertina. 'If what you are saying is right, he'll be getting off at the first station we stop at and doubling back . . . Bernay can't be far now . . . In fact . . .'

She broke off as the train entered a tunnel

151

and they began to lose speed.

Known facts or instinct: which to obey? Monsieur Pamplemousse closed his eyes and mentally tossed a coin.

By the time they emerged from the tunnel and they were entering the station, it had come down in favour of instinct.

Hastily following the others out onto the deserted platform only seconds before the train went on its way, he couldn't help but wonder what Pasteur would have had to say about it all. Not a great deal in its favour, he suspected. Seldom had his mind been quite so ill-prepared for what lay ahead.

CHAPTER SEVEN

'Bad news?' asked Amber, as Monsieur Pamplemousse returned after a brief chat with a member of staff at Bernay Station. From the look on his face, it was a self-answering question.

'You win some,' he said, 'you lose some. Corby did indeed get off the train here. It arrived at 10.20 and he was the only passenger to do so.'

He glanced at his watch. 'That was approximately an hour ago.'

Amber took in her immediate surroundings. 'At least Bernay is nowhere near the size of

Deauville. If he's anywhere around we're almost bound to come across him.'

'Looks deceive,' said Monsieur Pamplemousse. 'In terms of population, Bernay is roughly three times the size of Deauville. It happens to be more concentrated. Anyhow, that's academic. The bad news is he went straight out of the station and got into a taxi.'

'And they have no idea where he was going to?'

'None whatsoever, but I doubt if it was anywhere local. The first man I spoke to offered to help him with his bag, but he got short shrift. He simply got pushed aside without a word of thanks.

'All the man could say was he might have been heading back the way he came. He seemed in a hurry and he wondered if perhaps he had left something important behind. On the other hand, apparently a little way along the road there is a roundabout with multiple exits, so by now he could equally well be forty or fifty kilometres away in any direction you care to name.

Amber looked downcast. 'At least we know three things for sure,' said Monsieur Pamplemousse. 'He isn't making for Alsace-Lorraine, nor is he heading for Paris or the Channel Tunnel. Even if he originally intended to catch another train at Lisieux, he wouldn't want to go back there now for fear of meeting up with the *Chef de Gare*. Not much got past that gentleman.'

'What are his possible options?'

'From Lisieux? From Lisieux he could have picked up a train to Caen or Cherbourg. Opinions are divided, but the general consensus seems to come down in favour of Caen. Don't ask me why, apart from the feeling I have that unless you have a boat to catch, who would want to go to Cherbourg? They were beginning to clam up, wanting to know why I wanted to know . . . that kind of thing. Once a policeman always a policeman. I wasn't going to waste another €50 note on that one so, using my best bedside manner, I beat a hasty retreat.'

'You have one?' asked Amber in mock surprise. 'Beside manner, I mean?'

'Treating that remark with the contempt it deserves . . .' began Monsieur Pamplemousse.

Amber did her best to look contrite. 'I'm sorry. It's just that . . . all this "so near and yet so far" is getting me down. How about Caen? Do you think it's worth a shot?'

'You're forgetting one major problem,' said Monsieur Pamplemousse. 'My car is outside Lisieux Station. Ideally, we need to pick it up before we go anywhere else.'

Amber opened her handbag. 'This is beginning to feel like a trainspotter's day out.'

While she was unfurling the timetable, Monsieur Pamplemousse consulted his copy of

154

Le Guide.

'It seems to me,' he said, 'your friend Corby isn't the only one who has multiple choices. We may have missed out on the tractor-pulling contest—that takes place every June. Market day is on a Saturday—so that's out. But while we *are* here we could visit the museum and view their collection of old Norman furniture or, failing that, there is the Château de Baumesnil. It is said to be a masterpiece of the Louis XIII style, housing an extensive collection of seventeenth and eighteenth century books—some of the bindings of which are exquisite . . .

'On the other hand, if neither of those options appeals to you, why don't we take Pommes Frites for his morning constitutional? It will help clear our minds, and while we are at it we can look for somewhere to eat and plan our next move.'

'By the time we get back the taxi driver may have returned and we can find out where he went to,' said Amber.

'*Exactement.*'

'Masterly! But supposing he's got back and gone out again with another fare?'

'I slipped €50 to my first contact, asking him if he would keep an eye out for the driver and find out where he went to. He was feeling a bit anti-Corby anyway, so I'm sure he won't let me down. As an insurance policy, if he has to use his 50 for the driver, I've promised him

155

another. We can also leave our bags here. He said he would look after them.'

Refolding the timetable, Amber slipped it back into her handbag, then bent over her travelling case.

'It just so happens I brought these with me,' she said, removing a pair of Nike trainers.

'You know,' said Monsieur Pamplemousse thoughtfully, 'you are the nearest thing to the mother in *The Swiss Family Robinson* I have ever met.'

Privately he doubted if Madame Robinson had ever looked anywhere near as ravishing as Amber did when she bent over her duffel bag. It may have contained an answer to every eventuality likely to be encountered on a desert island, but even as a boy she had always struck him as being too good to be true. Certainly the thought had never kept him awake at night. Whereas, when Amber was bending over her case . . .

'That's something else no one has ever said to me before,' she said, using his shoulder as a prop as she began changing her shoes.

'First you praise my carbon foot print, then your boss says I'm a useful adjunct, now you liken me to a holier than thou white Swiss castaway of the female persuasion . . .' She offered him a cheek to kiss. 'If you're not very careful I shall be overwhelmed by it all, and then who knows?'

As they left the station, having deposited

156

their bags, Pommes Frites mentally added yet another item to his growing list of notes.

'I can see why Jay wouldn't want to hang around here,' said Amber. 'It isn't exactly his scene.'

She eyed the picturesque medieval half-timbered buildings as they entered the rue Gaston Folloppe. 'He would have been like a fish out of water. Can you imagine it?'

'Edith Piaf managed to cope with it,' said Monsieur Pamplemousse. 'Having been abandoned by her mother soon after she was born, she lived here with her grandmother over a brothel until she was fourteen. There is even a street named after her.'

'I doubt if Jay knows who she is,' said Amber. 'Anyway, she made good her escape, and how!'

They paused by an ancient bridge across the River Cosnier, and while Pommes Frites went to investigate a nearby weir, Monsieur Pamplemousse consulted his guidebook.

'I think we could be in luck's way again.'

'Not one from your private book this time?' said Amber.

Monsieur Pamplemousse shook his head. 'There is no need. Bernay seems to be one of those places the world has largely passed by. It even managed to survive all the devastation surrounding it in the Second World War. While the bombers were passing overhead it was covered by a blanket of thick cloud, so

157

they missed seeing a sitting target and went on to obliterate the centre of Évreux barely fifty kilometres away instead.'

'Life is basically unfair,' said Amber.

'And man's inhumanity to man knows no bounds,' said Monsieur Pamplemousse.

'Bernay may have hardly changed over the centuries, but someone on high must have had it in for Évreux in a big way. They say it burnt for almost a week.'

He snapped his book shut and set off back the way they had come, stopping outside a small restaurant on the right to study the menu.

'I think this will suit us admirably,' he announced.

Ushering the others inside, he seated Amber in a shady corner of a courtyard at the rear of the building and, leaving Pommes Frites in charge, returned to the front of the house to place their order.

'I have kept it simple,' he said on his return. 'Mussels to begin with. They may take a while to prepare—it's fairly labour intensive and the wife does all the cooking, but I have a feeling it will be worth the wait. I asked if we could skip the main course and they bring us a cheese board instead. To finish, there is *tarte aux pommes.*'

The words were hardly out of his mouth before the patron arrived with a tray of apéritifs: two glasses containing something

158

pale and chilled, and a plate of cheese *gougères*, the latter feather-light and clearly fresh from the oven.

'They must have seen us coming,' remarked Amber, after he had departed.

'Or going past the first time, more like,' said Monsieur Pamplemousse dryly.

He held his glass up to the light. 'I thought you might like to try this. Pommeau: two-thirds apple juice, one-third Calvados. It should go well with the *moules*.

'From all you have said,' he continued, as they settled back in their wicker-work chairs, 'I strongly suspect that by now your boss must be in a state of panic—going round and round like a fly caught in a jar. Here he is, on the run in a strange country, unable to speak the language and not knowing where to head for next. His biggest mistake so far is not to have taken advantage of your being here.'

Amber gave a shrug. 'That's Jay for you. He is basically a loner at heart.'

'In a way,' said Monsieur Pamplemousse, 'having seized on what must have seemed like a heaven-sent opportunity to escape the Mafia, there is no going back. I still maintain his best hope is to lie low for a while in some highly populated area, hoping the whole thing will blow over in time.'

'Then he will have another think coming,' said Amber. 'Once the Mob have someone in their sights, they never give up.'

'A chilling thought,' said Monsieur Pamplemousse.

'Perhaps we should start by asking ourselves where he wouldn't go?' suggested Amber.

'Or perhaps *oughtn't* to,' said Monsieur Pamplemousse. 'I agree with your suggestion that if he stays in Normandy he might end up for the time being somewhere near the sea. At this time of the year it would have the advantage of there being a floating population, but he would do well do avoid any of the big resorts boasting a casino . . .'

'How come most of them seem to be by the sea?' asked Amber. 'Don't they have any inland?'

'Blame the Emperor Napoleon,' said Monsieur Pamplemousse. 'In his wisdom he ordained they should only be allowed in places where there were thermal springs. His theory being that none but the very rich would stay in such places, and they could well afford to play.'

'Protecting the poor from themselves,' said Amber. 'Good old Napoleon.'

'That was the way his mind worked. Nowadays, any city with more than half a million inhabitants can have a casino, provided it supports the local arts.

'My point is that once again Corby needs to be careful since nobody is allowed into a casino without producing a passport.'

He broke off as the patron reappeared, carrying three large bowls. The first contained a steak *haché* for Pommes Frites, who attacked it with unbridled enthusiasm. The other two bowls were filled with pyramidal arrangements of tiny *moules* resting in their half shells rising out of a sea of liquid.

'It is the local version of what on the west coast is called *Mouclade*,' explained Monsieur Pamplemousse, after the patron had returned with two smaller finger bowls and a basket of fresh bread.

'Every coastal region of France has its own version of how it is prepared. Basically, the broth is made with white wine, saffron, onions, garlic and egg yolk, but because we are in Normandy they will have naturally added butter, cream and Calvados as a matter of course.'

'Naturally,' echoed Amber. 'If you ask me, it looks pretty labour-intensive for us to get through as well.'

They sat in silence for a while, concentrating on the task in hand.

'When Jay does fetch up, wherever it happens to be,' said Amber, dipping her fingers into one of the bowls of lemon-scented water, 'is there anything he can do to alter his appearance?'

'In the long term,' said Monsieur Pamplemousse, 'provided the money holds out, all things are possible. Surgery is obviously the main avenue. He could have a nose job, a hair transplant, cosmetic surgery on his cheek bones . . . but they all take time.

'Also, along with a new face, he will need the papers to go with it. Having the correct papers is essential in France, although once again, all things are possible if you know the right people.

'However, in the short term . . .' Carefully drying his fingers, he removed Corby's photo from an inside pocket and studied it. 'Going by your description of what he normally wears, I would say the first thing he should do is buy a new suit. I don't mean *new* new. An old one would be even better.

'Apart from trying to avoid any mannerisms that would give the game away, there isn't a lot more he can do at short notice.

'The days when a simple change of hat would have worked wonders have long gone. Nobody wears a hat these days unless it happens to be part of a uniform. Having one at all would be more likely to draw attention to him.

'Parting the hair on the opposite side to the one you normally do can be a help . . . or dyeing it.'

'He wouldn't know where to start,' said Amber. 'Jay isn't that domesticated.'

'In which case he might get himself a wig if he comes across the right shop. If he were in Paris there are dozens in the Boulevard Rochechouart area, literally every other shop in the Boulevard itself, but that's no help.

'Adopting a different walk can put people off the scent, but it's tiring and hard to be consistent, especially near the end of the day. He could have the heels on his shoes raised at any walk-in cobbler. Failing that, the stone-in-the-shoe trick works wonders.

'But of course voices are often a dead giveaway . . .'

'Try losing a Bronx accent,' said Amber.

'He could grow a moustache, and in the meantime perhaps get hold of a false one from a party shop to tide him over.

'Eyes are another problem area. Glasses can make a difference. I'm not talking dark glasses, which are often an object of suspicion, but any old pair of ordinary spectacles with the lenses removed. 'Perhaps a combination of all these things. I still maintain an old suit from a second-hand dealer would give him an entirely different image. It might do something for his body shape as well.'

'If he didn't make it with Waist Disposals Inc,' said Amber, 'I doubt it.'

Monsieur Pamplemousse was spared thinking up any more possibilities by the arrival of the cheese platter. It was accompanied by a bowl of unsalted butter, a selection of various other breads in a basket, and a bowl of fruit.

The patron went through the contents of the platter, tapping each one gently with the point of a knife. There was a generous wedge of

163

Camembert, a Livarot wrapped in its bands of striped raffia, a rich golden yellow Pont l'Évêque, and a heart-shaped Neufchâtel, all clearly in perfect condition.

Then, with a *'Bon appetit'*, he was gone.

'I am willing to bet none of them have ever seen the inside of a refrigerator,' said Monsieur Pamplemousse, after a closer inspection. 'It is the ruination of good cheese.'

'That may go for Normandy,' said Amber, 'but try telling it to a restaurant owner in somewhere like Las Vegas, where it gets to be forty degrees Celsius this time of the year.'

'Perhaps that is why Corby gave the one he went to such a bad write-up,' said Monsieur Pamplemousse, mildly surprised at her tone of voice.

Changing the subject, he moved a small bowl of greyish crystals closer to her. 'If you haven't come across this before, try some of it on the fruit. I guarantee you won't regret it. *Fleur de Sel.* Arguably the best sea salt in the world.'

'You never stop working, do you?' said Amber, as he scribbled a note on a scrap of paper.

'I'm afraid after a while it becomes second nature,' said Monsieur Pamplemousse. 'You should think yourself lucky that for once I don't have my notebook with me. The downside of my job is not having someone to share the good times with.

'Pommes Frites is a wonderful companion—
I don't know what I would do without him. He
has a good nose and he is a connoisseur of
many things, but as you have probably noticed,
fish is not one of them; neither is cheese, for
that matter. Give him a meal like the one we
had last night or a simple steak *haché* such as
he finished before we even began our *moules,*
and he is as happy as a pig in clover.'

'Nobody's perfect,' said Amber. 'I know one
thing: if I carry on like this, it's going to play
havoc with what you laughingly called my
carbon footprint.'

'You have a long way to go.'

'These things creep up on you,' said Amber.
'You two want to watch out—you don't want to
look like Jay. Not that he ever feels the need
to do much in the way of sharing.'

'The answer lies in moderation,' said
Monsieur Pamplemousse virtuously. 'It is the
best method of all . . . eat anything you like,
but do so in moderation. You can't go far
wrong.'

Helping himself to the butter, he was about
to spread a less generous helping than usual
over a wafer thin slice of walnut bread when
he felt a vibration in his jacket pocket.
Breaking off, he reached for his mobile.

'*Excusez-moi . . .*'

'Monsieur Pamplemousse?' The voice at the
other end sounded familiar.

'*Oui . . .*'

165

'We spoke earlier today . . .'

Monsieur Pamplemousse held his hand momentarily over the mouthpiece. 'It's the concierge again.

'How did you know my name?' he asked.

'I have not always been in Deauville, Monsieur,' came the response. 'For many years I held a similar position in Paris. At the time I often saw your picture in the journals, whenever there was an important case . . . most of all I remember the unfortunate affair involving the girls at the Folies. When you decided to take early retirement it was front-page news . . .'

Monsieur Pamplemousse raised his eyebrows heavenwards. Was he doomed to have it follow him around for the rest of his life?

He was about to remonstrate when the concierge, perhaps sensing he was on sticky ground, changed tack.

'I imagine Monsieur must now be working in a private capacity. They do say once a policeman, always a policeman.'

'They do indeed,' said Monsieur Pamplemousse wearily. True though it might be, it was also something of an irritation to have it repeated as a well-known fact from time to time.

'That being so, I thought you might like to know that when the person you were enquiring about checked out, he paid cash.'

'That is unusual?'

'At this end of the business and in Deauville of all places, it is practically unheard of. If it is a simple matter of money laundering, guests can use the casino. That is the easiest method of all—and the safest.

'Another thing which may be of interest to you, Monsieur, is that, in my experience, people who pay cash without apparently giving it a second thought don't usually assume the bill includes the cost of a lady's bathrobe. They are provided for the convenience of our guests while they are staying with us. If they wish to take one with them when they leave, they are on sale in the hotel gift shop along with other items of toiletry, perfume in particular.

'We pride ourselves on the fact that only the best will do. Christian Dior was born on the Contentin coast of Normandy. Granville is where he began life as a couturier—designing costumes for the annual Shrove Tuesday carnival celebrating the local fishermen's departure for long voyages. The gowns are sold in his honour.'

Monsieur Pamplemousse repeated a brief summary of the conversation to Amber.

She didn't pick up on the perfume so he was none the wiser what she was wearing.

'Give Jay his due,' she said. 'He knows quality when he sees it.'

'One other thing while we are talking,' said the concierge, resuming the conversation. 'All our guests enjoy the benefit of a leather folder in their room containing information about the hotel and the various amenities at their disposal, not only in the hotel itself, but in the whole area . . . it saves the desk clerk having to spend most of his time directing them to the Tourist Centre.'

'Don't tell me he took that too,' said Monsieur Pamplemousse.

'No, but I had the chambermaid check through the folder in the room he occupied, and she informs me that the section which normally holds a collection of brochures advertising various other resorts had been stripped bare.'

'And it would have been full when he arrived?'

'It is one of the maid's daily duties to make sure it is always kept up to date, Monsieur.'

'And they are all of places in Normandy? None for Brittany or anywhere else?'

'They are supplied by the Caen Chamber of Commerce,' said the concierge simply. 'Brittany is another world.'

'What places do they cover?' asked Monsieur Pamplemousse.

'Deauville itself, of course. And Caen *naturellement*; it is the cultural capital of the Basse-Normandie. The Normandy beaches, for the landing sites. Rouen for its cathedral, and as a gesture to *Les Anglais* in memory of Joan of Arc. Mont St Michel, because it is still there, as it has been for a thousand years. Bayeux, for its tapestry. Alençon, for its lace . . .'

Monsieur Pamplemousse thanked the concierge. The list sounded as though it might go on for ever and the more place names he heard the more formidable the task ahead of them sounded. He was getting value for his €50 after all. Quite how much was hard to say.

'It is my pleasure, Monsieur. It has been a great honour talking to you. If ever Monsieur intends visiting Deauville again . . . or if you require any further assistance, please do not hesitate to call me. As you are no doubt aware, in this business we have access to a great deal of information others might not be party to . . .'

He was quite right, of course. Concierges were a breed apart; members of a unique club that gave them access to secrets many outsiders would give their eye-teeth for. As discreet as any government security agency, they were walking mines of information accumulated over years of service and quicker even than the Internet; solving other people's problems was their *raison d'être.*

'God only knows what he needs with a bathrobe,' said Amber, when he told her. 'Walking off with anything that isn't screwed to the floor doesn't surprise me, but a bathrobe!

'Jay was weaned on hotel ashtrays, but he gave up on those a long time ago. The truth is, he is simply not geared to paying for things. I'm surprised he paid good money to stay at the hotel.'

'He would have been crazy not to,' said Monsieur Pamplemousse. 'It is as good a way as any of tracking people when you are on the move. That, and using credit cards.'

'Jay doesn't believe in credit cards,' said Amber. 'If you ask me, he must have brought a lot of cash with him. Or else he's been printing his own.'

Having no idea of the amount, Monsieur Pamplemousse decided not to tell Amber about the Director's cash on the nail payment.

'Either way,' he said, 'people often carry with them the seeds of their own destruction.'

'But why a lady's bathrobe?' persisted Amber. 'That's what gets me.'

'His mother?'

'You have got to be joking. Anyway, what makes it a lady's as opposed to a man's?'

'Perhaps he didn't even realise there is a subtle distinction. He simply grabbed it on the way out because it was handy. Would you like me to find out?'

Monsieur Pamplemousse picked up his phone and pressed the appropriate button.

'I am sorry to bother you,' he said. 'But can you tell me . . . what is the difference between a male and a female bathrobe?'

'About €50, Monsieur,' said the concierge. 'If you wish to order one for your wife the normal retail price is €350 for a gentleman's, so hers would be around €400. I am sure special terms could be arranged.'

'No, thank you,' said Monsieur Pamplemousse. At that price Doucette would fear the worst.

'But what's the difference?' hissed Amber, when he repeated it for her benefit. 'Ask if it's different material.'

'It is because of the hood,' said the concierge. 'We have found ladies who wash their hair regularly prefer them. That is why I think it must be a present for . . .' he allowed himself a discreet cough, 'a lady friend.'

'Pigs might fly,' said Amber, as Monsieur Pamplemousse thanked the concierge once again and terminated the call.

'I guess you were right the first time,' she said. 'He must have just made a grab for it out of force of habit. It's second nature to him. I doubt if he's ever paid for anything since he left nursery school in the Bronx and broke into the Principal's petty cash box with a hatpin. They wanted him removed on the grounds of their being unable to handle him.

'That night it got torched. Nobody knew whether it was Jay or his mother. She was the one who ended up doing time on account of her being older and should have known better.'

'If he is everything you say he is,' said Monsieur Pamplemousse, 'I'm surprised you still want to find him.'

There was another flurry of activity at the table as the dessert arrived.

'It is my wife's speciality,' said the patron proudly, while replenishing their glasses. 'Madame Morot's *Tarte aux Pommes Grand-Mère*. The secret is in the pastry, which I am not allowed to divulge, but I can tell you that the apples—the first of the season's Riene Rienettes, sliced as thin as a €1 coin—are covered with a glaze made from the sweetened peel, flavoured with cane sugar and Calvados.'

'I'm not sure I really want to know,' whispered Amber, when they were on their own. 'Pommes Frites wouldn't care to share mine, would he?'

'I hate to tell you,' said Monsieur Pamplemousse, 'but he doesn't do apples either.'

'To take you up on what you said just now,' said Amber, 'I guess the answer is Jay engaged me to look after him, as it were, and I don't give up that easily.'

'Corby's parents must have emigrated to the States when he was very small,' said Monsieur Pamplemousse, reaching for his fork. 'From what you said earlier, I assumed it must have been when he was much older.'

'I guess it must have been around the period of the Cold War, when everyone was getting twitchy about the possibility of there being a Third World War,' said Amber. 'One thing's

172

for sure. It was before my time.'

She hesitated. 'So, any ideas on where we go from here?'

'Having been born and brought up in the Auvergne,' said Monsieur Pamplemousse. 'I can't claim to be an expert on this part of the world, but . . .'

The conversation with the concierge had set his mind working. He was grateful for the offer of any sort of help. His only caveat was that by and large concierges were part and parcel of the upper echelons of the hotel world. If Corby had his wits about him, after his initial foray in Deauville he would give large establishments a wide berth.

'You've gone quiet on me again,' said Amber. 'What's going on in that mind of yours?'

'I was thinking of concierges,' said Monsieur Pamplemousse. 'I was thinking we need all the help we can get and they are not necessarily the best source in this case.'

In the old days he had been able to draw on a whole network of informers; people who made it their business to keep their ears to the ground, gathering up information and selling it on to the highest bidder; usually, but by no means always, the police. They were the gossip columnists of the underworld and often worth their weight in gold. For the time being, he was on his own.

'Perhaps the taxi driver will be back by now,' said Amber. She reached for her handbag.

'Meantime, before we do anything else, I must go in search of the bathroom.'

'I should come right out with it and ask for the *toilette*,' said Monsieur Pamplemousse. 'They won't know what you are talking about otherwise.'

He took advantage of being on his own for the moment to telephone Doucette.

Drawing a blank, he left a message on the answering machine, then sat back to make a few more notes. It had been a delightful meal. Simple, but beyond reproach and certainly worthy of a Wrought-Iron Table and Chair symbol alongside its entry in *Le Guide*. Anyone following the 'worth a detour' sign would be amply rewarded.

'Everything OK?' Amber reappeared, her long black hair now gathered bouffant style on top of her head.

'My mobile is beginning to glow red-hot,' said Monsieur Pamplemousse. 'But apart from that . . .'

'You're not going to believe this,' said Amber. 'But guess what I heard while I was in the you-know-where?'

'Try me,' said Monsieur Pamplemousse.

'There was a radio on in the kitchen. It must have been a local station because the announcer broke into the programme as though there was no tomorrow.

'As far as I could make out, the police are hot on the trail of someone they think may be

174

responsible for what he called "the recent bizarre events in Deauville".

'I didn't manage to get all of it, but I heard the patron and his wife talking about it afterwards.' She patted her hair. 'So I lingered as long as I could. Apparently the police have been setting up road-blocks in the area and some guy drove straight through one of them without stopping. They gave chase and they had almost caught up with the other car when both of them hit a sharp bend at speed. The police car managed to negotiate it, but the other driver carried straight on down a narrow lane and ran foul of a herd of cattle. Before the police managed to reach the scene he had made off, last seen disappearing into the St Gatien forest. Isn't that somewhere near the airport?'

'It was probably some poor innocent on his way to catch a plane and he panicked,' said Monsieur Pamplemousse. 'He must be wondering what hit him.'

'Poor innocent nothing,' said Amber. 'According to the radio the police have reason to believe he may be a terrorist.'

'"Have reason to believe,"' said Monsieur Pamplemousse, 'is usually another way of saying they are pretty darned sure, but they are working on it to get as much proof as possible before making an arrest. Charging someone with committing an offence is one thing, making it stick is another matter entirely.'

'They have to catch him first,' said Amber. 'There was no sign of the dog everyone's been talking about. The police have issued a warning saying not to go anywhere near him if he is sighted. He could be suffering from separation anxiety and may be dangerous.'

While Monsieur Pamplemousse took care of the bill, Amber folded her napkin neatly and began gathering her belongings.

Amid a plethora of *'bonnes promenades'* from the patron and his wife, they headed back the way they had come.

'That was a very professional-looking Bishop's Hat you made with your napkin,' said Monsieur Pamplemousse. 'I doubt if I could do as well.'

'So speaks the ex-detective,' said Amber lightly. 'Perhaps I've found my true vocation at long last. Besides, it was the least I could do after such a lovely meal.'

As they drew near the station, the driver of a parked car gave a toot and flung open his door. Leaving Amber to retrieve their cases, Monsieur Pamplemousse crossed over to the parking lot.

'You were making some enquiries about one of my fares earlier today,' said the driver. 'I'm not sure as it's right and proper to give information just like that . . .'

Monsieur Pamplemousse reached for his wallet.

'I drove him to Caen,' said the man. 'He

asked me to drop him in the centre. It struck me he didn't really know where he was going, so I left him outside the tourist office in the Hôtel d'Escoville.'

Monsieur Pamplemousse thanked him. It was progress of a sort.

'He didn't say where he was heading for next?'

'Not so as you'd notice. He hardly spoke, and when he did it sounded like Dutch to me. Or German. Could have been German.'

He slipped the note into an inside pocket. 'Can I take you anywhere? If it's local you can have it on me.'

'We need to get to Lisieux,' said Monsieur Pamplemousse. Out of the corner of his eye he saw Amber arriving back with their bags. 'And I'm happy to pay.'

This time Amber sat in the front. It was a long shot, but Monsieur Pamplemousse wanted Pommes Frites in the back with him. Corby would have been closeted in there for perhaps the best part of an hour. The chances were that he might have left some trace of his presence, enough to set an average bloodhound's nose twitching. Their olfactory powers were legendary, far in excess of any human measuring device, and Pommes Frites was no ordinary bloodhound. The problem would be trying to separate one scent from the many others there might be.

He pricked up his ears as he overheard

something the driver was saying to Amber. 'Chew, chew, chew . . . nothing but chewing all the way. Can't stand the stuff myself.'

'That's Jay for you,' said Amber over her shoulder. 'The bigger the problem the faster he chews. It used to be cigars before the No Smoking laws came in. Now he's God's gift to Wrigley's.'

Monsieur Pamplemousse raised his feet and saw what he was looking for straight away. Not just one, but several discarded wrappers.

He held one out for Pommes Frites to sniff, then carefully deposited the remaining ones in the lined inner section of his wallet.

'You are a wonderful man,' he said, handing the driver a note as he stopped outside Lisieux Station. 'Keep the change.'

'I don't think anyone has ever said anything like that to him before,' said Amber, as the driver shot off at high speed without so much as a backward glance. 'I must say you have a talent for that kind of thing.'

'*Merde!*'

'Now what?' she asked.

Monsieur Pamplemousse pointed towards the car park.

'My car isn't where I left it,' he said. 'In fact . . .' he scanned the rows of cars in vain.

Reaching for his mobile, he dialled a number. 'I think,' he said, 'as your friend Jay might say, it is high time we touched base.'

CHAPTER EIGHT

Having drawn a blank with the first number he dialled, Monsieur Pamplemousse flipped through his diary and found an alternative under 'Mobiles'. This time his call was answered almost immediately.

'Who is that?' asked an unfamiliar voice. 'What is it you require?'

'I was hoping to speak to a Monsieur Leclercq,' said Monsieur Pamplemousse. 'I'm afraid I must have the wrong number.'

'Pamplemousse!' exclaimed the Director. 'Don't tell me you are in Alsace-Lorraine already.'

'No, Monsieur. I am in Lisieux!'

'Lisieux?' repeated Monsieur Leclercq. 'Excellent! It could not be better.'

Apart from the fact that it was hardly the response he had expected, there was definitely something odd about Monsieur Leclercq's voice; what could only be termed a marked absence of its usual mellifluous tones in the lower register.

Monsieur Pamplemousse paused for a moment and put a hand over his right ear to shield it from the noise of a train pulling into the station.

'I am in Lisieux,' he repeated. It came out rather louder than he had intended.

'There is no need to shout, Pamplemousse,' barked the Director. 'I am not deaf.'

Monsieur Pamplemousse hastily sought to pour oil on troubled waters. 'If I may say so, Monsieur, I had difficulty in recognising your voice. It is amazing what a difference being in a darkened room can make to sounds. I suppose heavy curtaining absorbs the lower frequencies. That, and the thickness of one's duvet, of course.'

'Would that were the cause, Aristide,' groaned the Director. 'I am at my wits' end.'

Monsieur Pamplemousse decided to tread warily. Clearly, the change he detected wasn't entirely due to the acoustics of Monsieur Leclercq's bedroom. Perhaps it was simply a matter of his having climbed out of his four-poster bed on the wrong side that morning. It happened in the best of circles.

'I must say, Monsieur,' he continued, in an attempt to lighten the tone of the conversation, 'I had no idea Madame Leclercq was fond of budgerigars.'

'What *are* you on about, Pamplemousse?' barked the Director.

'I thought I heard chirruping in the background,' said Monsieur Pamplemousse. 'It reminded me of Madame Grante's Jo-Jo. As I recall, when Jo-Jo is "on song" you can hardly hear yourself speak, especially on days when it has overdosed on its millet spray.'

'And as I recall,' said the Director grimly,

'the operative word is *when*. It is an *oiseau* with a boundless lack of the basic social graces. Over the years it has acquired many of its mistress's less endearing qualities. When I last essayed a friendly gesture and poked my finger through the bars of its cage to bid it *bonjour,* it tried to peck the end off.'

'With great respect, Monsieur, I think it probably misread your intentions. If you remember, we were all on edge at the time because of the attempt to sabotage *Le Guide*. Animals and birds are very sensitive to undercurrents. They like everything to be in its proper place. The kidnapping of Madame Grante by that dreadful person who began by insinuating himself into her affections and then threatened to send parts of her anatomy through the mail unless his demands were met, must have been a traumatic experience for such a small creature, whose only major upsets until then had been the occasional late arrival of its iodised nibble.'

'Must you keep reminding me of these things, Pamplemousse,' groaned Monsieur Leclercq. 'It is an annoying habit of yours. Listening to you talk, anyone would think working for *Le Guide* was one disaster after another.'

'You must agree there have been rather a lot of narrow squeaks over the years,' said Monsieur Pamplemousse defensively. 'And we happen to be in the middle of one now, which is why I am phoning you.'

'Be that as it may, Pamplemousse, the sound you can hear is not that of a budgerigar, caged or otherwise. It is a *rouge-gorge*, and its beak is but a hairsbreadth away from my right ear. It keeps peering into the orifice to see what it can find. You would think it had never seen inside one before.'

'It probably hasn't,' said Monsieur Pamplemousse, relieved to be on common ground at long last. 'Robin Redbreasts are renowned for their inquisitiveness. They show no fear when it comes to investigating anything new. It is one of the problems inherent in leaving one's bedroom window open at night.'

His sense of euphoria was short-lived.

For some reason best known to himself, it sounded as though Monsieur Leclercq might be counting up to ten. Either that or he was temporarily short of breath. It was beginning to sound extremely laboured, like a steam engine nearing the summit of a steep incline.

'If you must know, Pamplemousse,' he said at last, 'the *oiseau* in question is hanging upside down from the branch of a bush, and the reason why my voice may sound odd is because at this moment in time I am lying in a ditch immediately below it. A ditch, moreover, which is not only full of thistles, but is within striking distance of my own home. I have only to cross the road—'

'It may be a silly question,' broke in

Monsieur Pamplemousse, 'but if that is the case—'

'Why do I not climb out of the ditch and do just that? Is that what you are saying, Pamplemousse?' responded Monsieur Leclercq. 'For a start, you never know who you might meet on the way, but over and above that I happen to be well and truly wedged. I fear it is the trapdoor syndrome in your play all over again, exacerbated by the fact my muscles are not yet fully recovered from yesterday's debacle. There are parts of my anatomy that have been lying idle for a good many years and they are currently a matter of considerable concern to me.'

Monsieur Pamplemousse felt tempted to suggest it was no wonder the *rouge-gorge* was having a ball. It was to be hoped its excited tweets did not reach the ears of other redbreasts in the surrounding area, many of whom would probably welcome any kind of diversion in their otherwise humdrum daily routine.

'There are those, like my wife's sister, Agathe, who believe the body is full of poisonous sacs,' he said, by way of comfort. 'Little containers brimful of noxious substances. Left to their own devices, they pose no threat. However, if she, or in this case he, meaning your good self, indulges in too much unaccustomed exercise, jumping up and down, *par exemple*, or even lying in a ditch, they are liable to spill over into one another's territory with dire results.'

'There are some things I would rather not know, Aristide,' said Monsieur Leclercq. 'I have enough problems as it is.'

'Can you not telephone for help, Monsieur? You need only dial 17 and I am sure the police will be with you in no time at all.'

'That is the very last thing I wish to do,' groaned Monsieur Leclercq. 'It would be akin to stepping into a lion's den at feeding time without so much as a can of spray-on instant sedative at my disposal.'

'But, Monsieur, you must take my word for it. The police may have their faults—no one is perfect—but at such times—'

'The truth of the matter is—' the Director broke off for a moment and took a deep breath. 'I have a confession to make, Aristide. One which is for your ears only. To put it bluntly and not to mince words . . . I am on the run.'

'On the run, Monsieur? From a *rouge-gorge*?'

'Worse, Aristide, far worse. From the local *gendarmerie*, no less.'

'But—'

If the Director was experiencing difficulty in clarifying his situation, Monsieur Pamplemousse felt totally at a loss for words. To put it mildly, he was momentarily stunned. For all his faults, Monsieur Leclercq had a strong sense of right and wrong. He was normally a paragon of virtue, an upright citizen of the very first echelon. It was hard to imagine anyone less likely to be on the run from the police. He racked his brains to think what could possibly be serious enough to warrant his hiding in a ditch.

'I am not hiding, Pamplemousse,' groaned the Director in response to his question. 'I fell into it by accident while making a final dash for home. Until then I was not even aware of its existence.

'It is a sorry tale, I fear. But to begin at the beginning, I am glad you have telephoned because you will have to be apprised of all the facts sooner or later.

'It so happened Chantal was driving into Deauville to do some shopping this morning. Knowing how much your old 2CV means to you, and not wishing it to fall into the wrong hands—a passing collector of ancient artefacts seizing his chance, perhaps—she offered to go via Lisieux and drop me off at the *gare*, so that I could drive it back home and leave it in our garage for safc-keeping.

'For that reason, and for that reason alone, Aristide, I rose from my sickbed. I felt it was the least I could do in return for all the hard work you put in on making the play such a success. Please be assured I shall not rest easy in my bed until it has been fully restored.'

Monsieur Pamplemousse felt himself

growing more and more confused.

'It is most kind of you, Monsieur, but I thought you said you were lying in a ditch.'

'There you go again, Pamplemousse,' barked Monsieur Leclercq. 'Splitting hairs as usual!

'I was speaking metaphorically, of course. The fact is . . .' once again the Director seemed to be having difficulty in finding the right words. 'The fact is, Aristide, and it grieves me beyond measure to tell you this, but it may take a while to restore your *Deux Chevaux* to its former glory.'

'Someone has driven into it?' asked Monsieur Pamplemousse uneasily. 'It is getting harder and harder to find the parts.'

'No, Aristide, nothing as simple as that. Very much the reverse, in fact. For the time being it is lying on its side in a ditch halfway between here and Lisieux.'

'Lying on its side?' repeated Monsieur Pamplemousse. 'In a ditch!'

'Half in, half out,' Monsieur Leclercq hastily corrected himself. 'I am told panel-beaters can do extraordinary things these days. In the meantime, I am sure it is perfectly safe. Given the circumstances, I imagine the area will have been cordoned off with that ghastly coloured tape they use for crime scenes, and doubtless someone will have been left on guard while photographers and fingerprint experts do whatever it is they have to do. You would know far more than I do about what goes on. I shudder to think what will happen if the media get hold of the story.'

'I think, Monsieur, you may find they already have, always assuming it is the same car, that is. There was an item on the radio at lunchtime today.'

'I doubt if there are many cars lying on their side in the area,' said the Director.

'I still don't understand how it happened,' said Monsieur Pamplemousse. 'The 2CV was designed and built in the days when Citroën insisted on having a wheel at all four corners of their cars, consequently they are renowned for their stability. I have never heard of anyone managing to overturn one. It simply isn't possible.'

'It is if you are going at speed down a narrow country lane and you encounter a herd of cows going in the opposite direction,' said the Director. 'For such large animals they are remarkably slow on the uptake. As for your 2CV having a wheel at all four corners, I fear it is deficient in that respect. Its quota has been reduced to three. The offside front one collided with a trec and became detached. For some reason, when I attempted to apply the brakes my right foot found itself entangled with a pile of waste material under the seat.'

'Did you discover what it was?' asked Monsieur Pamplemousse nervously.

'There was no time,' said the Director. 'As the car came to rest I climbed out of it and, despite the mooing coming from all around me, I detected the sound of an approaching siren. At which point, I must confess I panicked and made a run for it.'

Monsieur Pamplemousse breathed a sigh of relief; it was one less hurdle to clear.

'If I may ask—' he began.

'Why was I travelling down a narrow country lane at speed in the first place?' surmised the Director. 'I had no other choice, Aristide. Until that moment I had been driving along the D279 in a civilised manner, familiarising myself with the vagaries of a strange car whilst at the same time manoeuvring it around the kind of obstructions one encounters more and more in this day and age. For example, I was scouring the dashboard for some means of controlling the air-conditioning, and as one of the knobs came away in my hand I only just managed to avoid a row of cones protruding halfway across the road.

'Moments later, what I took to be a road hog of the very worst kind tried to overtake me. He kept flashing his lights and the more he flashed them, the faster I went. I didn't realise until it was too late that it was a police car. Quite simply, we came to a sharp bend in the road. I carried straight on and they went round it.

'I am very much afraid, Pamplemousse, there is something sadly amiss with your power assisted steering.'

'That is not possible, Monsieur.'

'Nonsense,' said the Director. 'Nothing is impossible in this day and age.'

'It is if you don't have it in the first place,' said Monsieur Pamplemousse.

'I count myself lucky to be alive . . .' continued the Director. He broke off. 'Did I hear you say you don't have power steering, Pamplemousse?'

'That is correct, Monsieur. Nor, for that matter, do I have air conditioning, other than by opening one of the windows.'

'Were they not listed as optional extras when you bought the car?' asked the Director.

'There were no optional extras on the 2CV, Monsieur. In those days what you saw was what you got. That was the whole point of it. The list of all the things it didn't have was a major selling point. Besides, it was all I could afford at the time.'

'When this sorry business is over and the police have completed their findings, I strongly recommend you have power steering installed,' boomed Monsieur Leclercq. 'Lack of it must make going round corners extremely hazardous.'

'I usually rely on the camber of the road, Monsieur. In bad cases, when there isn't one, I depend on Pommes Frites for help. The most recent example was when you needed me in a hurry and I had to drive all the way from Rodez in the Midi-Pyrénées to Paris before lunchtime—a distance of some six hundred kilometres. I put the car into many a four-wheel slide going round corners, and he came in extremely handy. Being unusually sensitive to changes in motion, he simply closes his eyes and uses his weight to good effect. He was in his element.'

This reference to the most recent near-disaster—the one which, in effect, brought Corby into the picture in the first place—did the trick, as he hoped it might. Monsieur Leclercq hastily changed the subject.

'Did you say you heard the news on the radio at lunchtime, Aristide?'

'It was a little before one o'clock, Monsieur. We were in Bernay.'

'One must be thankful for small mercies, Aristide.' The relief in the Director's voice was palpable. 'I have already spoken to the Regional Deputy, who happens to be an old friend of mine—we attended the same *grand école* together. He agrees that, since the police will have undoubtedly identified the ownership of the car on the National Computer by now, for your own sake as well as for the sake of all those concerned, *Le Guide* and myself included, the best course of action is to allow them to draw their own conclusions and assume it was stolen. That is provided, of course, I am able to reach home unseen.'

It took Monsieur Pamplemousse a finite amount of time to digest the information. It was no wonder the Director was unwilling to risk being spotted crossing the road. The whole area was probably alive with police by now.

'Silence is golden, Aristide,' said Monsieur Leclercq.

'And withholding evidence is a serious offence, Monsieur,' countered Monsieur Pamplemousse.

'But if you are not asked, Aristide . . .' persisted the Director. 'If you are not asked and you produce proof you were in Bernay at the time, that should be sufficient.'

Now who is splitting hairs? thought Monsieur Pamplemousse.

'I have a receipt for the meal,' he said. 'We began with mussels—the local version of *Mouclade*. Then we had a superb cheese board, followed by a speciality of the *maison*; *Tarte aux Pommes,* as the patron's step-grandmother made it. I strongly suspect the recipe must have been handed down over the years.'

'Typically Norman,' said the Director approvingly. 'I trust you made notes, Aristide.'

'I did indeed, Monsieur.'

'Excellent!' exclaimed Monsieur Leclercq. 'Now, once I have managed to release myself, all I have to do is return home unseen and we have nothing to worry about.'

'Can you not phone your wife, or a member of staff?'

'Chantal's mobile is switched off. If she has

191

gone shopping for clothes I doubt if she will be back much before midnight. It *is* nearing the Season in Deauville, after all. In any case, ignorance is bliss and I would rather she remained ignorant of the facts—I shall be saved hearing of nothing else during the months to come.

'As for the staff . . . they have been given the day off to recover from yesterday's extravaganza. In any case, their being local means I cannot possibly involve them. Tongues will undoubtedly wag. It will be all round Deauville before you can say "*tout suite*". '

'Is there no one who can help you?'

'Sister has returned to Paris,' said Monsieur Leclercq. 'I strongly suspect she overdid it on the refreshments. Her hand was extremely unsteady when she examined me for bruises. Rambaud has stayed on to do a few odd jobs, but he doesn't have a mobile, so there is no way of contacting him. Even if there were, trying to explain matters to him would take forever. He would probably end up bringing me a prawn sandwich like he did in the theatre.

'We must have someone working in Normandy but they are probably much too far away by now to be of any help.

'The truth is, Aristide, other than your good self, there is no one I can turn to. That is why I said your still being in Lisieux, whatever the reason, is excellent news. I suggest you take a taxi and get the driver to drop you off at the front gates of my home. Tell him you think the walk to the house will do you the world of good, which I am sure it would. I did it myself once soon after we moved in. Most invigorating.'

'How will I find you, Monsieur?'

'Wait until the driver is out of sight, and then simply dial my number,' said Monsieur Leclercq. 'You should hear it ringing somewhere amongst the brambles. I will leave it unanswered so that it will guide you to where I am lying.

'And Aristide . . .'

'*Oui*, Monsieur?'

'Please try not to be too long about it.'

'I suppose you can't really blame the police for jumping to the wrong conclusion,' said Amber, when Monsieur Pamplemousse relayed the news to her. 'A notice on the windscreen saying "Beware of the dog", along with what looks like a kit of parts for a secret agent in the boot, plus a pile of assorted unmentionables under the front seat . . .'

'And the Director's fingerprints over all the controls,' said Monsieur Pamplemousse. 'How is he going to get out of that one?'

'Don't forget mine,' said Amber. 'I might have been a back-seat driver, or worse. If the police put all those things together they could be looking for a spy who is also a sex maniac operating a mobile brothel on the side.'

'One way or another, we had better move quickly,' said Monsieur Pamplemousse. 'Free the Director and then get the hell out of it. If they once pull us in for questioning it could go on for days.'

'I don't see why we can't leave him where he is,' said Amber. 'Tell him there wasn't a taxi to be had. I'm game for most things, but I draw the line at brambles.'

'We can't just leave him,' said Monsieur Pamplemousse. 'He's probably stuck in a storm ditch. There might be a sudden downpour. There often is in these parts.'

'That should free him if nothing else does,' said Amber unfeelingly.

'Suppose it doesn't?'

'Someone in the village is bound to go past at some point. By the sound of it he can't be very far from the road.'

'That is the last thing he wants. I know how his mind works. The news will spread like wildfire. Apart from anything else, bang goes his chance of being mayor.'

'What's so special about being a mayor?'

'In France they represent the last vestiges of local power,' said Monsieur Pamplemousse, rising to the Director's defence. 'They are all things to all men; ombudsman, righter of wrongs, guardians of their local realm, rolled into one. They bring about a sense of community that would otherwise be lacking.

Besides, they have all manner of perks. For a start they get to sit at the head of the table wherever they go.'

'And that matters?'

'It does to the Director. It means a great deal to him. It is second in importance only to avoiding loss of face, and as things stand he is in great danger of losing out on both counts.'

'Silly me,' sighed Amber. 'I guess it takes all sorts. We had better look for a taxi.'

'While you do that,' said Monsieur Pamplemousse, 'I must make another call.'

Something the Director said had set his mind working. It was such an obvious move he could have kicked himself for not thinking of it before.

His call was answered on the first ring.

'Congratulations on your performance, Véronique,' he said. 'I trust your stage husband is not giving you too much trouble.'

'Nothing I can't handle,' said Véronique. 'Anyway, I'm thinking of giving up treading the boards and retiring while I am at my peak. Parts like that are not likely to come my way again in a hurry. What really decided me is I am running out of garlic.'

'Who do we have in the North at the moment? I am thinking of Normandy in particular.'

There was a moment's pause.

'Truffert?' repeated Monsieur Pamplemousse. 'Couldn't be better. Any idea where he is?'

'His last report came from the Caen area. He went straight there after the party. Now he's on his way to Bayeux. Can I help at all?'

'Would you be kind enough to ask him to ring me as soon as possible?' said Monsieur Pamplemousse. 'I'm not sure where I shall be, so if you give him my mobile number he can get me on that.'

'Your carriage awaits, Monsieur,' said Amber, as he terminated the call.

'I thought you all went on holiday at this time of the year,' she continued, as he brought her up to date on their way to the waiting taxi. 'It felt like it at the end of the play. Everybody seemed to be heading off in different directions.'

'So they were,' said Monsieur Pamplemousse. 'Half were going off on holiday, the other half were going back to work. *Le Guide* has to strike while the iron is hot. Most of the coastal regions, the Channel and the Atlantic ones in particular, virtually close down during the winter months. Hotel owners seize the opportunity to take a holiday themselves, or more often than not these days they have a second hotel in one of the ski resorts.

'Truffert was brought up in this part of the world, so he'll have as good an idea as anyone where Corby might end up. *And* he is on the spot.'

'Let's hope,' said Amber, accepting the taxi

driver's offer of a front seat.

Monsieur Pamplemousse and Pommes Frites were very firmly relegated to the back of the car. Clearly a man of few words, but with deep-seated likes and dislikes, the driver, feeling the latter breathing heavily down the back of his neck, turned up the volume of his radio, rendering the exchange of any pleasantries out of the question for the time being.

Monsieur Pamplemousse concentrated instead on the back of Amber's neck, reflecting how often in life relationships blossomed and bore fruit while those involved were more than content to see only a fraction of the whole. Both sides of any partnership, marital or otherwise, tended to show their best side at the beginning of a courtship, and it was in the nature of things for people to zoom in on what had attracted them in the first place.

Amber was a case in point. Seen at close quarters, the back of her neck was eminently kissable. You could understand anyone falling for it. But it was only a minute part of the whole. He wondered what she would be like when roused. Quite a fireball, most likely.

Following the direction of his master's gaze, Pommes Frites was having similar thoughts. Although, in his case the idea of a good lick was as far as it went. Highly regarded in many areas as a token of love and a panacea for all ills, his recent singular lack of success with

Monsieur Leclercq put him off the idea.

The object of their thoughts, on the other hand, remained inscrutable. Head down, lost in thought, fingers in her ears, Amber looked as though she was content to while away the journey in contemplation of her navel.

En route they passed, and were themselves passed, by several police cars, but otherwise the road was remarkably clear of traffic. News spread fast.

Halfway to their destination, his telephone rang and he did his best to answer it.

Truffert sounded out of breath. 'I got your message,' he said. 'Trouble?'

'Nothing life-threatening,' said Monsieur Pamplemousse. 'What the boss would call an *Estragon* situation,' he added.

'One of those!' groaned Truffert. 'Tell me the worst—if you can make yourself heard above the noise. It sounds as though you're in a night club . . .'

'It is not an ideal moment,' agreed Monsieur Pamplemousse. Shielding the mouthpiece of the phone, he responded as quickly and as succinctly as possible.

'My bet would be on Mont St Michel,' said Truffert, without any hesitation. 'Apart from Paris, it has a higher number of visitors per annum than anywhere else in France. Around 3.5 million. That's aside from its normal quota of pilgrims. I'll look in my diary and check on the state of the moon.'

'Why?'

'It affects the tides. The really high ones bring visitors pouring in by the coach load.'

'Would Corby know all this?'

'Any hotel brochure will mention it. I remember catching sight of him leaving after the show. He looked pretty cut-up about something. Is there anything else I should know about him?'

'He drinks Coca Cola for medicinal purposes and he uses what's called a swizzlestick to get rid of the bubbles.'

Truffert sounded dubious. 'I guess they've tracked people down with less, but you should know. Is it important?'

'Very,' said Monsieur Pamplemousse.

'How about the police?'

'It wouldn't be a popular move,' said Monsieur Pamplemousse. '*Anonymat* and all that.'

'*D'accord!*' said Truffert. 'I'll keep my ears to the ground and get in touch again if I hear anything.'

'We shall most likely be in Caen by then ...'

'If you are,' said Truffert, 'I can give you the name of a good restaurant near the Marina. They do superb *escalopes de veau*. The chef uses a cupful of vermouth instead of the usual cider. It makes a change.

'By the way, have you read the reviews of the play?'

'I haven't even seen a journal,' said

199

Monsieur Pamplemousse.

Truffert gave a chuckle. 'Just you wait!'

'Jesus!' said Amber, as they alighted outside the entrance to the Leclercqs' summer residence and the taxi went on its way. 'I was looking at the floor mat and counting up to ten most of the way. It didn't exactly have WELCOME written on it, or if it ever did it wore away a long time ago.'

'It only confirms what you said earlier,' replied Monsieur Pamplemousse. 'It takes all sorts. And one way or another, taxi drivers manage to embrace most of them.'

He took out his mobile. 'Now for the moment of truth.'

'Watch out!' hissed Amber, as an unmarked police car came around the bend and headed towards them.

She was a split second too late. At almost precisely the same moment as Monsieur Pamplemousse pressed the button, the car drew up alongside them and two policemen climbed out.

In what he was later to consider one of his finer moments, he converted the dialling motion into holding the mobile up as though taking a photograph, then slipped it into an inner pocket and put a finger to his lips.

'We're looking for a man,' began the older of the two. 'Rough diamond. Like a gorilla. Stop at nothing . . .' He glanced down at Pommes Frites. 'Got some kind of giant

200

mastiff with him. By all accounts it would make yours look like a Dandie Dinmont.'

'Ssh!' said Monsieur Pamplemousse, as the sound of ringing came from some brambles on the other side of the road. 'It might fly away.'

'That's a bird?' said the younger of the two.

'Sounds more like a telephone to me,' agreed the older man.

'*Exactement*,' said Monsieur Pamplemousse. 'That is how the lesser spotted wurzel got its nickname—"the telephone bird". Its call is music to an ornithologist's ears. It is what distinguishes it from all other birds.'

'I can't wait to tell them back at the station,' said the number two.

Monsieur Pamplemousse made a sucking noise between his teeth. 'I would much rather you didn't,' he said, warming to the subject. 'It is almost extinct. If word gets out the place will be swarming with people and we shall risk losing it altogether.

'We are researching material for a possible television programme on its breeding habits. Unless we find a mate for it, that will be the end of the line.'

'If you do, and they get together,' said the number two, 'will it make a noise like the engaged signal?'

'I thought I'd seen you before,' said the senior of the two, glaring at his assistant. 'There used to be a lot of husband and wife teams on television. I remember Armand and

Michaela Denis for a start. They were my favourites. That Michaela was something else again.'

'Must have been before my time,' said the younger of the two. 'Never heard of them.'

'Everything's before your time,' said the older one.

He turned to Monsieur Pamplemousse. 'If you have finished, Monsieur, we would be delighted to give you and your partner a lift back into Lisieux.'

Monsieur Pamplemousse did a repeat performance of his sucking through the teeth noise, only this time with more feeling. Any moment now and the Director would get impatient and start shouting.

'I would be very grateful if you could take *mademoiselle* to the *gare*. I have a few things to tidy up . . .

'I can phone for a taxi,' he added, for Amber's benefit.

Clearly the idea appealed to the younger of the two. He instantly rose to the bait. 'I've never met an ornithologist before,' he said to Amber. 'You're not at all how I pictured one.'

'I'm sorry about that,' said Amber, fluttering her eyelashes.

'Don't be sorry,' said the policeman. He held the door open for her. 'Hop in.'

'I will be with you as soon as possible, *chérie*,' called Monsieur Pamplemousse.

Amber blew him a kiss as she climbed into

202

the back seat of the car.

Not to be outdone, Monsieur Pamplemousse executed a deep bow and reached for his handkerchief. He was about to use it to wave *au revoir* when something about the feel of it warned him against the idea. It was a narrow squeak and no mistake, but by then he had other matters on his mind.

As the car disappeared around the bend, a familiar voice rang out.

'Pamplemousse! What on earth is going on? Where are you?'

*   *   *

'How are your researches on the lesser spotted wurzel going?' asked Amber when they eventually met up at the *gare* in Lisieux.

'Alas!' said Monsieur Pamplemousse. 'I fear the worst.'

'And the object of the exercise?'

'Mission accomplished,' said Monsieur Pamplemousse. 'The bird has been returned to his nest and is as well as can be expected. How about you?'

'Mine actually wanted to demonstrate his handcuffs on me!' said Amber. 'I doubt if he will try them out on anyone else for a while. Anyway, where to now?'

'Caen,' said Monsieur Pamplemousse. 'The sooner we get out of here the better.'

Amber reached into her handbag and

produced two tickets. 'I was hoping you might say that.'

'You have a receipt?' asked Monsieur Pamplemousse.

'I was rather hoping you might say that too,' she said.

Shortly before their train arrived, the *Chef de Gare* appeared, clutching his clipboard and beaming instant recognition.

'Monsieur, Madame,' he said. 'And how was Paris?'

'It went like a dream,' said Monsieur Pamplemousse. 'So much so, it feels as though we were never there.'

'I trust you will find Caen to your liking, Monsieur.'

'You don't happen to know the trains to Mont St Michel, do you?' said Monsieur Pamplemousse.

'From Caen, Monsieur?'

'From Caen.'

'It is *très difficile*. The most direct route is to take the intercity train to Rennes and alight at Pontorson. That is the nearest stop for Mont St Michel.'

Monsieur Pamplemousse thanked him. 'That shouldn't be too difficult.'

'Alas, Monsieur, they are few and far between. On Mondays there is one leaving at 05.42 and another at 07.13, but with that you have to pre-book a taxi between Coutances and Foligny. There are none mid-week. Most of the traffic is geared for the weekend outings. On Fridays there is one at 16.43. On Saturdays, Sundays and fête days there is the 09.13, which stops at Pontorson, and another at 14.13. There is even one at 17.13.

'When you get to Pontorson you can take a bus or a taxi to Mont St Michel. I strongly recommend you take a taxi . . . it is so much quicker. The company is called 'Allo Raymond and the number is 02-99-27-10-10 . . .'

'What's the betting Raymond is a cousin,' said Amber, as they settled back in their seats and the train slid gently out of Lisieux station. 'Twice removed, but never far away.'

'In this part of the world,' said Monsieur Pamplemousse, 'it is more than likely. Families are very close-knit.'

'Anyway,' said Amber, 'I feel better now. If he says the timetable is *très difficile* it must be darned near impossible for ordinary mortals like me to work out. How he can reel out all those times is beyond me. The man is a walking encyclopaedia. He must eat, sleep and dream timetables.'

'A true railwayman of the old school,' said Monsieur Pamplemousse. 'Besides, I suspect he has been asked the same question many times before.'

'I don't even know what day it is,' said Amber.

'By the look on Pommes Frites' face,' said Monsieur Pamplemousse as he joined them, 'you are not the only one. He is wearing his "where do we go from here?" expression.'

'I guess he's not into predestination,' said Amber. 'I mean, don't you ever get the feeling that there are some things in life that are meant to happen, come what may?'

'There are times,' admitted Monsieur Pamplemousse, 'when everything seems to depend on being in a certain place at a certain time. In retrospect, you don't even remember why you were there. Even simple things like the Director deciding to move my car, which in turn led me to phone Truffert, a call which gives me cause for hope . . .'

'Isn't that leaving too much to chance?'

'I prefer the word "probability",' said Monsieur Pamplemousse. 'Professional gamblers don't believe in chance—that's in the lap of the gods. If they hit a bad run they stop playing for a while, knowing that the law of averages will be on their side and in the meantime the odds in their favour are piling up.

'Is it all pre-ordained? Who knows?'

'Then again, there is the way we met,' persisted Amber. 'I mean, I doubt if I would be sitting on this train with you if it hadn't been for Pommes Frites.'

'That too . . . !' Monsieur Pamplemousse's voice sounded guarded even to himself. 'We shall have to wait and see. Patience is the key word.'

'There speaks your true ornithologist,' sighed Amber.

CHAPTER NINE

Monsieur Pamplemousse made himself comfortable in a window seat opposite Amber.

'It seems to me,' he said, 'that somewhere along the line Corby has either been ill-advised, or he has unwittingly boxed himself into a corner. Whichever it is, it could be to our advantage.'

'Meaning?'

'Assuming he is heading for Mont St Michel, the fewer ways there are of getting there the easier it will be for us to catch up with him, so unless he finds some method of transport other than the train—'

'I can't picture him taking a coach, if that's what you're thinking,' said Amber. 'There would be too much socialising. Comfort stops—that kind of thing. You know what they're like these days. He wouldn't go for that kind of thing.'

Monsieur Pamplemousse didn't know, but he could guess.

'Given that he doesn't drive, and taking a taxi that distance would be too conspicuous a luxury, he is really left with no alternative . . . unless, of course, he gives up on the whole idea.'

'Jay is a typical Scorpio,' said Amber. 'Once he has decided on a course of action he doesn't give up easily.

'He is also a New Yorker by adoption, and you know what the song says: "If you can make it there you can make it anywhere." You don't do that by sitting on your backside in Caen.'

'Well, seeing as today is Thursday and there won't be any more trains to Mont St Michel until tomorrow,' said Monsieur Pamplemousse mildly, 'he doesn't have much choice in the matter.'

'Is that so bad?'

'From his point of view it isn't exactly ideal. If you thought the streets in Deauville were long and straight, wait until you see Caen. He was probably picturing an ancient city full of narrow alleyways and dark corners, whereas nowadays it is quite the opposite.'

Gathering his thoughts as they emerged from the long tree-lined cutting which made up the first part of the journey, he gazed out at the passing scene: thatched half-timbered houses and farm buildings dotted the landscape, mostly in splendid isolation from each other.

Occasionally he caught sight of a group of single-storey cottages in the distance, clustered round a larger building boasting a steeple.

Picket fences divided one piece of land from another, and here and there neatly stacked piles of wood stood in readiness for the coming winter. A Norman dovecote built of flint and stone, large enough to house a sizeable family, came and went. Groups of creamy-white dairy cattle lay basking in the afternoon sun.

'I hate to say it,' he said, 'but I think it's going to rain.'

'Rain?' repeated Amber unbelievingly.

'The cows are all lying down,' said Monsieur Pamplemousse.

'You believe in that kind of thing?' Amber looked up at the cloudless sky. 'If you ask me, they're probably suffering from heat stroke, but what do I know?'

'It is a matter of instinct,' said Monsieur Pamplemousse. 'Cows often sense things long before we do.'

'Well, if they are right,' said Amber, 'it will mean a shopping expedition. I'm equipped for most things, but not rain in July.'

They sat in silence for a moment or two.

'What can we expect when we get to Caen?' asked Amber.

'How long is a piece of string? Its main claim to fame is tripe: *tripes à la mode de Caen.*'

'If you are looking for an excuse not to take me out tonight,' said Amber, 'carry on talking. The very thought puts me off.'

'In the mid-west of America they get around the problem by calling it "Sonofabitch stew",' said Monsieur Pamplemousse. 'It contains all the working parts from the inside of a calf: heart, liver, tongue, sweetbreads, brain, plus something called the "narrow gut" connecting it all with the fourth stomach.'

'See what I mean?' said Amber. 'That kind of concept reminds me of another sonofabitch, name of Jay Corby. Anyway, aside from Caen's main claim to fame resting on a ruminant's basics, what else is there I should know?'

'Being a lady of fashion,' said Monsieur Pamplemousse, 'there is that well-known English dandy, Beau Brummel. Towards the end of his life, having gambled away all his fortune in the UK, he fled to France to escape his creditors and ended up in Caen, where he became British Consul. That lasted all of two years. He eventually died in a charitable asylum.'

'I am beginning to wish I hadn't asked,' said Amber.

'Along with Pommes Frites,' said Monsieur Pamplemousse, 'I am a picker-upper of unconsidered trifles. His occasionally stick in his gullet, whereas I store mine away for future reference. You never know when they might come in useful.'

Clearly, it wasn't one of those occasions.

'It can't all be doom and gloom,' said Amber. 'There must be an upside to it all.'

'Caen is lucky to be still there at all,' said Monsieur Pamplemousse. 'In 1944 more shells and bombs landed on it in the space of two months than Hamburg received in the entire war.

'All of which is a bit ironic seeing that in 1074 King Henry the First and William the Conqueror signed a treaty called "The Truce of God", specifying future wars could only be fought on certain days of the week and then only at certain seasons of the year.'

'I guess nothing is for ever,' said Amber. 'But why? I mean, why Caen in particular?'

'The Germans decided to defend it because it happened to be an important transport hub. Not only were there road and rail links in all directions, but in spite of it being a good twelve kilometres from the sea, there was a thriving dock area reached via a canal. It was a godsend to the Allies when it came to landing supplies.

'The upside of it all is that having been left with three-quarters of their city razed to the ground, the inhabitants of Caen had to start all over again from scratch, and in so doing they created a blueprint for what many other cities all over the world are only now beginning to aspire to. It has a superb transport system including a network of trams that run every three minutes, wide pavements almost everywhere, a pedestrianised shopping centre, and plenty of off-street parking.

'Here and there traces of the old city remain: William the Conqueror's Chateau, which is practically indestructible; and by some miracle its two main *abbayes*: the Abbaye-aux-Hommes and the Abbaye-aux-Dames.'

'His and Hers abbeys sound like something Nieman Marcus would have in their Christmas catalogue for the person who has everything,' said Amber.

'I wouldn't let anyone in Caen hear you say that,' said Monsieur Pamplemousse. 'You will see what I mean when we get there. It may have a race course in the middle of it, but places to hide away in are thin on the ground.

'If he has any sense, Corby will keep a low profile. Since the end of the war it has become a Mecca for Anglo-American veterans visiting the Normandy landing beaches. Given the amount of publicity he enjoys back home, he will stand a good chance of being recognised by one of his fellow countrymen.'

'Do you think we should start looking where the taxi driver dropped him off?' asked Amber. 'He may be holed up somewhere near there.'

'Truffert reckons that if Corby is planning to move on, he would look for a small hotel near the *gare*,' said Monsieur Pamplemousse, 'and I would go along with that. They are more likely to be geared to catering for the passing trade: reps and the like. It depends how much luggage he has.'

'A carry-on bulging at the seams,' said Amber. 'I asked the driver while you were busy looking for gum wrappers in the back of his cab.'

'What Corby wouldn't have known,' said Monsieur Pamplemousse, 'is that the *gare* is on the other side of the River Orne, to the south of the city.

'It is only a few minutes' tram ride away from where he was dropped off, but since he would have no idea which one to take or how to pay for a ticket, most likely he would have set off on foot following the signs. In which case, he would have had a good twenty minutes' walk ahead of him.'

'Perhaps it'll teach him to stick to pocketing ashtrays in future,' said Amber. 'How about we do a quick recce of the hotels near the station when we get there?'

Monsieur Pamplemousse glanced at his watch. It showed a little after 17.30.

'It is late in the day for that kind of thing.'

He looked out of the train window. The picturesque scenery showed signs of giving way to more commercial activities . . . present day Caen was home not only to a flourishing steel industry, but also electronics in its many forms. The number of lines and waiting train sets grew more noticeable by the minute.

'I think we should keep a low profile for the time being. We don't want to trigger off alarm signals. Who knows? Truffert may come up with something.'

'Isn't that kind of a long shot?'

'Long shots are better than nothing at all,'

said Monsieur Pamplemousse, 'and I am all for letting other people help do some of the work for us if they can.

'There isn't a police force in the world that doesn't rely to some extent on what are euphemistically called "informers", but they are paid according to market value. In most other fields people are only too happy to do it for free. They love a good gossip. You want to know about the latest fashions? Go shopping in the Avenue Montaigne in Paris. Clocks and watches? Visit the Horloge area of Paris. They all have their own grape vines, and the hotel world is certainly no exception.'

'Not even a little recce in the meantime?' asked Amber, fluttering her eyelashes.

Monsieur Pamplemousse shook his head. 'Assuming Corby is heading for Mont St Michel, our best bet is to be at the *gare* in good time for the 16.43 tomorrow afternoon. You can bet your life on one thing. If he has gone to all this trouble to avoid being found we don't want to frighten him off at this stage and lose him altogether.'

'I must say I could use a bit of space,' said Amber reluctantly. 'Somewhere with an overnight laundry service wouldn't come amiss.'

'That being so . . .' Monsieur Pamplemousse opened up his copy of *Le Guide*, ran his eyes down the list of possible options, and marked two with outstretched fingers.

'Your choice.'

Amber closed her eyes and ran a hand lightly down his arm. 'As the saying goes, it isn't exactly rocket science, but . . .'

Reaching his hand, she carried slowly on down to his forefinger and pressed the tip.

'Pommes Frites *will* be pleased,' said Monsieur Pamplemousse. '*Chiens* are welcome. The other one doesn't take dogs, which would be a major problem because his inflatable kennel is still in the boot of my car.'

'Don't tell me I've missed my chance yet again . . .' sighed Amber, as they drew into the arrival platform.

While she disappeared to freshen up after the journey, Monsieur Pamplemousse rang the hotel to make sure they had rooms.

Having received an affirmative, he moved behind a pillar and signalled Pommes Frites to take up a position some distance away in order to divert her attention. For no particular reason, but purely on a whim, he had it in mind to take a photograph of Amber in an unguarded moment.

It might appeal to the editor of *l'Escargot, Le Guide*'s house magazine. There were those among his colleagues who would appreciate such a variation to pictures of the 'dishes of the day', which so often graced the front cover.

'I tell you one thing,' said Amber on her return, blissfully unaware of his machinations, 'that bathroom is palatial with a capital P, the best 20 cents worth I've had in a long time.

'And I'll tell you something else,' she continued, as they headed for a taxi rank in the Place de la Gare. 'I see what you mean about the wide-open spaces. Jay's going to love this place like a hole in the head.'

The hotel was at the city end of the Avenue du 6 Juin; as near to the spot where Corby had been dropped off as it was possible to be. Monsieur Pamplemousse didn't comment on the fact in case Amber took it into her head to dive straight in, but it was also close to the Tourist Agency.

He suddenly felt in need of thinking time.

It struck him quite forcibly that the situation was reversed. Until now, it had been a case of the hunters and the hunted. Helped by a head start, Corby's constant movements and counter-movements, motivated as they were by the strongest of all forces—self-preservation—had successfully kept him ahead of the game.

Were Monsieur Pamplemousse in his shoes, he would be keeping a weather eye open for any pursuers.

Given Pommes Frites' stage appearance coupled with his previous success in the Director's food tasting exercise, Corby was almost certain to recognise him. It would be a miracle if he didn't. But as far as he, personally, was concerned, they had met face to face only very briefly at the tasting. In any case, he could well be in Caen as part of his work for *Le Guide*, so he wouldn't necessarily constitute a serious threat.

Amber was another matter. If Bernard's report of the way Corby had greeted her at the Leclercqs' party was anything to go by, she would certainly come under the heading of those he would rather not see. Maybe he was frightened she might give the game away when she got back to the States . . .

'I suggest that after we have checked in, you have a bath and relax. We can meet up in the lobby and go somewhere for a drink before dinner,' he said, as they alighted from the taxi.

'Set that to music,' said Amber, 'and it could make the Top Ten anywhere in the world. Right now, a bath is my number one. How about you?'

'Certain among us are in need of a promenade,' said Monsieur Pamplemousse.

Pommes Frites pricked up his ears, and sure enough, no sooner had they checked in to the hotel than they were on their way out again, heading not towards a nearby stretch of water, which would have been his own first choice, but to a shop of some kind.

There were times when it was hard to follow the working of his master's mind. Once inside, Monsieur Pamplemousse went straight up to a large counter in the centre, removed a picture from his wallet, and showed it to a girl. She shook her head, and having shown it to several of her colleagues, all of whom reacted in the same way, she pointed to some shelves lining the walls.

Having waited patiently while his master looked through various bits of paper, rejecting some, keeping others, much to Pommes Frites' relief they retraced their steps towards the venue of his choice. Why they couldn't have gone straight there in the first place was beyond him.

The central part of the vast Quai Vendeuve fronting the south west side of the equally spacious Bassin St Pierre was reserved for the parking of cars, and it was more than half full, but from a dog's point of view the rest of the area had a lot going for it.

The far side was lined with boats, and in his experience people on board boats were often more than generous to anything on four legs. Then again, on the near side there were lots of small restaurants, many of which were either open or were getting ready for the evening rush.

Sniffing the air, Pommes Frites licked his lips at the thought of the many possibilities that lay ahead. The nicest part of all, of course, was having his master to himself. Not that he was of a jealous disposition. The bond between them was as firm as a rock, but he was only too well aware that the two of them together was one thing; adding a third could make it totally different, especially when the newcomer was female. At such times his master's attention was apt to wander. He always came back in the end, of course, but the bit in the middle could be a worry.

Unaware of Pommes Frites' thought processes, and having registered the fact that the Quai was rather quieter than he remembered it—probably because it was holiday time and many of the 30,000 or so students at Caen's ancient university must be absent—Monsieur Pamplemousse was keeping an eye open for the restaurant Truffert had recommended. Dinner that evening could be the last good meal they would enjoy for a while, and he already had a place in mind, but it would be no bad thing to have somewhere in reserve.

For reasons he would have found hard to explain to anyone else, he sensed a change in Amber. Something was amiss. A certain hardness just below the surface had crept in, almost as though she were running on auto pilot.

Loudier would have put his finger on the cause straight away: lack of proper communication. In his opinion it was one of the major problems in today's world. Despite all the means people had at their disposal, or perhaps because of them, there was no such thing as a real conversation.

People automatically make the dangerous assumption that what they are saying is crystal clear to whoever it is they are talking to, whereas more often than not they are on an entirely different wavelength, their minds elsewhere, or, worse still, they've got hold of completely the wrong end of the stick.

He was fond of instancing Lawrence Durrell's 'Alexandria Quartet', where the four leading characters became involved in the same series of events, but when it came to be their turn to relate what had happened, each of them saw it in an entirely different light.

Monsieur Pamplemousse decided that, had he been awarding himself marks under the heading of 'communicating with Amber', 5/10 would have been a fair assessment, with the added comment 'must try harder'.

Not for the first time he found himself wondering if perhaps underlying it all Corby meant more to her than she was prepared to admit. It was a subject he was determined to bring up over dinner that evening.

At which point he registered the first of some heavy spots of rain, and with Pommes Frites leading the way, they hurried back to the hotel.

Both literally and metaphorically it put a damper on things. Neither he nor Amber were remotely prepared for it.

Having abandoned the idea of a pre-dinner aperitif followed by a leisurely stroll to a restaurant awarded a Stock Pot in *Le Guide*, his insistence on all three of them sharing the hotel's sole remaining umbrella didn't help matters.

'Goddamn cows!' said Amber. 'If Caen is so ahead of the game in everything else, why can't they make use of them as part of an early warning system?'

'It doesn't work that way,' said Monsieur Pamplemousse. 'For a start they wouldn't want to lie down on the sidewalks, and anyway, it's a chicken and egg situation—'

'Don't tell me they get in on the act too,' said Amber.

'You're not really a country person, are you?' said Monsieur Pamplemousse.

'Too damn sure I'm not,' said Amber, as she stepped in a puddle.

'This could be our last good meal for a while,' said Monsieur Pamplemousse. 'We would be well advised to make the most of it.'

'Mont St Michel is not on your preferred list?'

The flourish of the hand accompanying his heartfelt *'Non!'* while he paused to shake the worst off the umbrella before entering the restaurant didn't help matters.

Dodging one of the spokes, Amber stepped in another pool of water.

'So what's wrong with Mont St Michel?' she asked when they were seated.

'Once upon a time,' said Monsieur Pamplemousse, 'there was a wonderful young lady called Annette Poulard, who was to become world famous for her omelettes. It was

221

said that there was nothing quite like them. Some vowed it was because they were made with fresh cream, others maintained she beat the yolks and the whites separately before combining them in the pan. Pillars of society flocked to La Mère Poulard: the British Royal Family; the American and French Presidents of the day; the Rothschilds and the Rockefellers . . .

'She died in 1931, taking her secret with her to the grave and, gastronomically speaking, Mont St Michel has never been quite the same since.'

'Is it that bad?'

'Let us just say the world itself has changed. Nowadays the restaurants tend to cater for the tourist trade. Most people are only there for the day and they prefer to spend their time sightseeing rather than eating.'

Laying aside the menu, Amber gave him the go-ahead to order for them both. Clearly, from the way she was clutching her evening bag, her mind was on other things.

'I suggest we begin with *cocquilles Saint-Jacques D'Étretat*,' said Monsieur Pamplemousse. 'It is made with mushrooms, shallots, crème fraiche and Calvados.'

'Does everything you eat in this country get named after someone or something that happened God knows how long ago?' said Amber.

It wasn't a good start. It would serve her

222

right if he had ordered tripe and given it another name.

'Whenever possible,' said Monsieur Pamplemousse. 'It is what sets places apart from each other and engenders a feeling of pride. It isn't a case of living in the past, but rather of not forgetting it. The whole history of a town is often laid out for you in its street names; not just battles and the generals who fought them, but the Edith Piafs of this world get remembered as well. They are all part of our heritage.

'One of the longest avenues in Paris is named after Antoine Parmentier, who popularised the humble potato. There is a marble statue of him on the Metro station bearing his name. He is clutching a basket of potatoes under his arm while offering one to a passer-by. *Crêpes Suzette, Poire Belle Helene, Pêche Melba* . . . they are all a form of celebration.'

'But does it make things taste any better?' asked Amber.

'No, but it adds enormously to my enjoyment,' said Monsieur Pamplemousse. 'One of the great joys of working for *Le Guide* is that it has enabled me to get to know my own country. When I open a bottle of wine it isn't simply the name on the label, or the year, it is the very land itself which sets my taste buds throbbing; the *terroir*. As for this dish . . . what do you think of it?'

Amber had to admit it was delicious.

'Étretat is famous not simply for its shellfish,' said Monsieur Pamplemousse, 'but also because over the years its huge arched cliffs have been an inspiration to so many writers: Maupassant, Alexandre Dumas, Victor Hugo, André Gide . . .

'In much the same way, Cabourg is renowned not simply for its wonderful beach, but because it is where Proust spent his holidays watching the world go by, and where he wrote *A la Recherche du Temps Perdu.*'

'I bought a Madeleine the other day,' said Amber. 'It came in a plastic wrapper I had to tear open with my teeth. I wonder what he would have thought of that?'

'I imagine it would have confirmed his belief that we should cherish things past,' said Monsieur Pamplemousse.

'It was in a New York deli,' said Amber.

'Ah!' said Monsieur Pamplemousse.

He paused while the table was being prepared for the main course: a coil of *boudin noir* resting on a bed of golden brown apples. Doused with a glass of Calvados, it arrived wreathed in flames.

'No doubt the *boudin* is from Montagne-au-Perche,' said Amber dryly. 'Isn't that where the pigs feed off windfall apples?'

'Bonus points!' said Monsieur Pamplemousse. 'In the old days every town and village had its specialities, and not simply in the way of food.

224

Lyons was famous for its locksmiths, Normandy for its horse dealers; Thiers became noted for cutlery, Meru for making dominoes out of cows' tibias; Barthelemy-d'Anjou cornered the market in public urinals ... I could go on ...'

'I'd rather you didn't,' said Amber. 'It might put me off the *boudin*.'

For the second time Monsieur Pamplemousse took in the way she kept reaching for her evening bag. That he didn't have her undivided attention was patently obvious.

'Does finding Corby mean so much to you?'

She relaxed her grip, but didn't let go of it.

'I'm sorry. I'm being an ungrateful bitch. It's just that I hate the uncertainty of it all. I guess I can't come to terms with the possibility that even now he might be somewhere around. On the other hand, you said yourself that Caen is a transport hub. He could have taken a boat to England, a plane to almost anywhere, a train—'

'It would take a team of investigators to sift through all the options,' said Monsieur Pamplemousse, with rather more conviction than he actually felt. 'All we can do at this stage is keep playing hunches built on our assessment of where he *wouldn't* go and hope they are right.

'For example, taking a boat isn't as straightforward as it might sound. I checked

225

up soon after we arrived here. As for flying anywhere . . . he's had ample opportunity to do that from day one, but he hasn't taken it up.'

For dessert, he had ordered a warm concoction made up of alternate layers of quartered pears and confectioner's custard in a brioche case.

'It is called timbale *Brillat-Saverin* after the famous chef,' he explained.

'You don't give up, do you?' said Amber.

'It is the Capricorn in me,' said Monsieur Pamplemousse. 'Scorpios may not change their mind, but Capricorns get what they want in the end.'

'You sound like a Canadian Mountie,' said Amber. 'Following that line of thought. What do you reckon my star sign is?'

'If there were such a body,' said Monsieur Pamplemousse, 'it would be an Enigma. You are a definite enigma.'

'Why is it that other people's lives are so much tidier?' asked Amber.

'Perhaps they aren't really,' said Monsieur Pamplemousse. 'They just seem to be.'

Amber glanced down at Pommes Frites. Somehow or other he had managed to acquire a lump of confectioner's cream on the end of his nose.

'If there is such a thing as a second life and I have any choice in the matter, I wouldn't mind coming back as a mutt.'

'You could do far worse,' agreed Monsieur

Pamplemousse.

'Would you take me for walkies occasionally?' asked Amber.

'I might. It would depend very much on the weather.'

'You could keep a cow in the back yard,' said Amber.

'The nicest thing about Pommes Frites,' said Monsieur Pamplemousse, 'is that he is a dog for all seasons and not just a fair weather friend. True unquestioning love and devotion is what sets animals apart from humans, although you have to earn their respect first.'

In Pommes Frites' case he could have pointed to a recent habit he had developed, that of checking the ends of his master's trouser legs before they went out in the morning.

But that was a secret between the two of them. No doubt it would come to an end once they were safely back home.

CHAPTER TEN

The phone call Monsieur Pamplemousse had been setting so much store by came through at just past two o'clock the following afternoon.

With several hours to fill before the departure of the train to Mont St Michel, and in between a series of heavy showers, they had gone their separate ways for a while; Amber to do some shopping, and after investing in a pac-a-mac and a notebook, he had set out with Pommes Frites to explore what was left of the old city.

'Funny thing,' said Truffert. 'I have absolutely no idea where your man is at this moment in time, but I think I know where he's been.

'Traces have been found in one of the hotels right opposite the *gare*. Not one, but two empty Coca Cola cans in the waste basket. Brought in ones—nothing to do with the hotel. It doesn't run to bedside fridges. Circumstantial evidence, I agree . . . but the description fits, so I had a chat with the management and they said they would hold back on doing the room until you get there. But I should hurry; they weren't too sold on the idea.

'The reason I got to hear about it is because apparently whoever stayed there left the bath in such a filthy state it's the talk of the rue Jules . . . They have all been to see it.'

'Are you saying he has checked out already?'

'Early this morning. Nobody knows where he went to, but it could be worth following up. Have you got a pen handy? I'll give you the details . . .

'I guess from all you have said he is most likely still in Caen, but if you don't manage to pick up the trail I still think it would be worth

228

the drive to Mont St Michel.'

'It would be if I had a car,' said Monsieur Pamplemousse.

'You don't have a car?' repeated Truffert. 'Don't tell me it's given up the ghost at long last!'

'It is a sad story,' said Monsieur Pamplemousse. 'It might make you want to cry.'

'Don't spoil my day,' said Truffert. 'I'm on my way to Carantec—'

'Patrick Jeffoy's hotel?'

'The very same. Just checking to make sure it rates two Stock Pots.'

'I can still taste his *Homard bleu* . . .'

Truffert gave a mock yawn. 'It's all right, I suppose. If you like that kind of thing. I may go for the *tête de veau rôtie* myself . . .

'Listen, I know a good place to stay in Mont St Michel. It's laid back from the main ones, but there is a good view of the bay and its comings and goings. I can phone ahead if you like . . .

'It will be one up on Corby. He'll be lucky to get within sight of the Mont itself this time of the year. You need to book up months ahead in the Season, and come August he could have a major problem.'

Monsieur Pamplemousse thanked Truffert, double checked on the name of the hotel in Caen—the street opposite the *gare* was awash with them—wished him luck in the arduous work that lay ahead of him, then went in search of Amber.

He found her in the rainwear department of Galeries Lafayette, looking as near to a million dollars as it was possible to be in a raincoat. He decided the casual way the belt was fastened had a lot to do with it. Her time in France had not been wasted.

A short walk from the Galeries they picked up a tram heading south.

'Another first,' said Amber, as Monsieur Pamplemousse validated their tickets.

'From the way Truffert was talking I should prepare yourself for yet more very shortly,' said Monsieur Pamplemousse.

The management of the hotel turned out to be a lady of uncertain years and even more uncertain temper. 'He's got big paws,' she said accusingly, as Pommes Frites bounded up the stairs ahead of them, leaving a trail of wetness.

Monsieur Pamplemousse didn't rise to the bait. Any mention of carbon footprints would have fallen on deaf ears. Instead, he waited until they were shown into the room they had come to inspect.

Once inside it he removed one of the chewing gum wrappers from his wallet and offered it up for expert assessment.

Having sniffed his way round the room, Pommes Frites found several screwed-up wrappers under the bed, followed by two more alongside the Coca Cola cans in the waste bin.

'It has to be Corby,' murmured Monsieur Pamplemousse.

He and Amber both stood back and watched while Pommes Frites did several more circuits of the room before heading for the bathroom, where he concentrated first of all on the basin and then the bath. It was hard to say which of the two was in a worse state; they were both all-over black.

'I don't get it,' said Amber, looking over Pommes Frites' shoulder as he placed his paws on the edge of the bath and peered at it.

'Jay may be a hundred per cent copper-plated shitsky, but he is spotlessly clean with it. Like with his clothes. It may look as though he wears the same outfit every day, but that's because he buys them at wholesale rates.'

In retrospect she had to admit that asking the manageress if the bathroom had been clean in the first place was a big mistake. The torrent of abuse couldn't have been worse had she cast aspersions on the woman's personal hygiene.

'Pardon me,' said Amber. 'But it looks like the inside of a coal mine. What could he possibly have been up to?'

As though in answer to her question, Pommes Frites made his way back to the waste bin and returned almost immediately with the remains of a cardboard packet.

'Black dye,' said Amber, examining what was left. 'Industrial size by the look of it. I guess

231

your theory must be right. If Jay used it all up on his hair it's no wonder the bathroom is in such a mess.'

'I'm glad you're happy,' said the manageress. 'All I know is this room has to be made up before the maid goes off. She's over the time limit as it is already, and that costs. It's going to take a lot of elbow grease. Who's going to pay for it? That's what I'd like to know.'

Monsieur Pamplemousse reached for his wallet, and having thanked the woman for her trouble, palmed a similar amount to the room maid as they passed her waiting impatiently behind a trolley in the corridor.

'I think you've scored there,' said Amber, as they took their leave. 'Not once, but twice over! I'm jealous.'

'I shan't lie awake tossing coins,' said Monsieur Pamplemousse.

'Talking of which,' he looked at his watch. 'Since it is almost a quarter to three, why don't we have a snack in the *gare*? It's hardly worth going back to the hotel and we can check out the geography of it all.'

'That's another of your big words,' said Amber, as they set off across the square.

'It is a big *gare*,' said Monsieur Pamplemousse. 'And there are only two of us.'

'Two?' She looked down at Pommes Frites.

'I think this is one of those occasions when the second part of the phrase *"C'est interdit! Mais toleré!"* won't necessarily apply. Pommes

Frites and I had better keep together as much as possible, otherwise he may get seen off the premises.'

'I feel contaminated,' said Amber, as they entered the *gare*. 'Do you happen to have a twenty cent piece?'

Monsieur Pamplemousse obliged, and while she was gone he took stock of the surroundings.

Although plate-glass windows and doors ran the entire length of the main building, most people seemed to be making use of the same double doors they had just entered by. It made sense, as they were the nearest ones to the bus and tram stops.

Just inside to his left, there was the entrance to a sit-down cafeteria. Further along, to his right and on the street side, there was a booth serving coffee, sandwiches and other light refreshments.

After the hotel manageress, the lady in charge of the booth was like a breath of fresh air, although clearly she ran a tight ship. The coffee machine gleamed, and on the wall behind her, chocolate bars stood to attention alongside bottles of mineral water and fruit juice.

A marble-topped counter ran the length of it before disappearing round the far end, creating a small sit-down eating area.

He ordered two espresso coffees and a selection of pastries, before staking a claim on

233

two stools. Relatively secluded, it afforded an ideal view of the area outside, covering the arrival and departure of trams, buses, taxis, and anyone on foot.

Securing the approval of the lady behind the counter, he left Pommes Frites in charge of the seating and set off on a quick voyage of discovery.

The entrance to the main waiting area was a little way along on the left. Immediately inside and again on the left there was a *tabac* with an impressive array of newspapers, magazines and souvenirs. Facing it was a sizeable seating area for waiting passengers, and beyond that again, past various vending machines and display boards, he could see the booking area and an open-plan enquiries counter.

The exit door for those boarding the trains was in the middle of a wall facing him in the waiting area. There was a large electronic display board high up on the wall listing arrival and departure times, and on either side of the door stood the usual ticket validating machines.

Through the opening he could see a vacant *quai* and, to the right, a downward flight of stairs, which presumably led to a tunnel serving the rest of the five or six *quais*. There was an empty set of carriages in the furthest one away. Given that Corby's train started from Caen, it might well be his, although it wouldn't be shown on the board until nearer the departure time.

So far, so good. Like everything else in present-day Caen, it was all very spacious, but there were precious few places in which to keep a low profile.

Having completed his tour of inspection, Monsieur Pamplemousse returned to the refreshment booth, arriving there at almost the same moment as Amber.

He couldn't help noticing she was carrying what he had come to think of as her evening bag. Perhaps she was looking forward to a celebration? He had given up trying to read her mind.

'What do you picture happening when we meet up with Jay?' she asked, pulling up a stool next to his. 'I mean, it would be nice to have first go if that's OK with you?'

'Feel free,' said Monsieur Pamplemousse. 'All I need to know is what his intentions are regarding *Le Guide*. Is it good news? Or is it bad? If, due to a misunderstanding, it is the latter, I must try and talk him out of it.'

He gave her a brief rundown of his findings.

'The train to Rennes starts from here, in fact, it may already be in place. When the time for boarding is announced I suggest you go straight to the *quai*. If it's other than one that is immediately outside the door it will make things easier. You can wait in the tunnel and check all the passengers as they go by.

'I don't think there are any other ways he

can use to give us the slip, but you never know. My guess is he will make a last-minute dash for it, so stay where you are until the train pulls out. The only downside is that he may not realise he needs to validate his ticket before boarding the train. That could be his downfall, and may be ours too.'

'How come?' said Amber, 'Surely it isn't the end of the world.'

'When the ticket collector comes round on the train and sees it isn't date-stamped, he will either have to pay a hefty fine on the spot, or if he can't or he kicks up a fuss, he could find himself put off at the next station. Ignorance of the rules is no excuse.

'Pommes Frites and I had better stay up here and keep an eye out for late arrivals.'

Amber glanced across at the waiting room. It was growing more crowded by the minute. 'They can't all be going to Mont St Michel, can they?'

'There is another train scheduled before the 16.43,' said Monsieur Pamplemousse. 'That ought to account for quite a few. As for the ones who are still waiting for the train to Rennes, there are a good few stops on the way.'

'Who goes to Mont St Michel anyway— apart from people on the run like Jay?'

'School children as part of their History lesson . . . Religious groups on a pilgrimage . . . The world and his wife . . .'

236

'And their offspring, too, by the look of it,' said Amber. 'Although I don't see any buckets and spades.'

'French children don't build sandcastles,' said Monsieur Pamplemousse. 'They go shrimping. Sandcastles are the prerogative of the English. What do American children play at?'

'I have no idea,' said Amber. 'Baseball, I guess.'

'*Vive la différence!*' said Monsieur Pamplemousse.

'What draws people to Mont St Michel is its uniqueness . . . the sheer grandeur of it—especially when seen from a distance. Half of those going there don't explore the cathedral itself, it is too daunting; they simply gaze at it in awe and try to do it justice with their digital cameras.

'Others go there simply to witness the tremendous tides that roar in at the speed of a galloping horse, although even that isn't what it was. The harbour has been gradually silting up over the centuries and there is a long building programme in place, diverting the waters of a river to try and clear it by natural means.'

'Don't they read the papers?' asked Amber. 'If they put it on hold for long enough, global warming should do it for them.'

Sensing a return of the chippiness he had experienced the previous evening, Monsieur

237

Pamplemousse drained his coffee cup and brushed aside some cake crumbs. He was beginning to feel uneasy himself. It must be catching.

He looked at his watch. 'As soon as the next train comes in I suggest you grab a seat as near to the exit as possible. If you want something to hide behind until the last minute, why don't you buy a journal at the shop just inside?

'In the meantime . . . *bonne chance.*'

Boarding for the Rennes train began twelve minutes before the departure time. He caught a brief glimpse of Amber making for the door ahead of the rush, before she disappeared down the stairs leading to the tunnel.

At 16.43, dead on time, the train left and quietness descended.

There was a long wait before she reappeared. Her face said it all.

Pommes Frites looked first of all at Amber, then at his master, and let out what was meant to be a comforting whimper, but somehow it was much louder than he had intended.

'I hope it isn't something he ate,' said the lady in charge of the bar.

Amber held up a folded copy of an American newspaper she had been carrying. It was open at the leisure page. At the end of a restaurant review there was a short note: AJ CORBY IS CURRENTLY ON HOLIDAY.

'The heavy type must be their way of saying they have no idea where he is either.'

'What does the "A" stand for?' asked Monsieur Pamplemousse out of curiosity.

'Arsehole!' said Amber.

'Ooh la, la!' came a voice from behind the counter.

*   *   *

'So you think we should go through the whole Goddamn routine again for the 09.13 tomorrow morning?' said Amber, over dinner that evening.

'And, if necessary, the 14.13 and the 17.30 too,' said Monsieur Pamplemousse. 'Don't forget it is a Saturday service.'

'And if he isn't on any of those?'

'We do exactly the same thing on Sunday and keep our fingers crossed he doesn't leave it until the 05.42 on Monday.'

'Jesus!' said Amber.

'As someone once said in a different context regarding old age,' said Monsieur Pamplemousse, 'it's better than the alternative.'

'I'm not even sure about that any more,' said Amber.

'The thing about the present situation,' said Monsieur Pamplemousse, 'is that we don't really have an alternative. Speaking personally, I have always believed in following my instincts. They have served me well over the years.'

'I wish I could say the same about mine,' said Amber.

'I have a sneaking feeling Corby is still around,' said Monsieur Pamplemousse, 'and I doubt if it is because he has fallen in love with Caen. It may even be a matter of instinct with him, too. Perhaps he is simply playing it safe for a couple of days in the hope of putting people off the scent. Who knows? I can't think of any other reason.

'In the meantime, I see the patron is waiting in the wings with pencil poised, so I suggest we take advantage of Truffert's recommendation and order the escalopes of veal for the main course, and perhaps to start with, how about a lobster bisque? It will go with the weather.'

He looked out of the window. Despite the time of the year, it was already starting to get dark. Umbrellas were being unfurled yet again.

Amber glanced over her shoulder while he was placing the order. 'Why are you always so right?'

'In my last job,' said Monsieur Pamplemousse, 'you didn't win any medals for getting it wrong, and much the same goes for my present one. You develop a sense of smell . . .'

'Since you are so obviously dying to ask,' said Amber. 'It's Chanel No 19. "Fresh, light, adventurous, delightful" or so the adverts say.'

'That depends a great deal on the person

wearing it,' said Monsieur Pamplemousse. 'If I may say so, three out of four isn't bad.'

She looked at him quizzically. 'Now you've got me at it. Which particular one am I lacking?'

Monsieur Pamplemousse was spared having to answer by a flurry of table-laying, followed almost immediately by the arrival of a soup tureen. As the patron removed the lid with a theatrical flourish, the smell that rose from the creamy rich contents enveloped them.

Their reaction didn't pass unnoticed by a small group outside who had been studying the menu board. Monsieur Pamplemousse raised his glass to them as they trooped in.

'Opting for a window table has its advantages,' he said. 'You get good service for a start. The patron's performance wasn't entirely for our benefit; it was timed to perfection and it did the trick.

'It also means I can play the favourite game of food inspectors everywhere: "Shall we? Or shan't we?"

'What makes non-regulars go into a restaurant? You can almost see their minds working as they study the menu outside and weigh up the pros and cons before peering inside. Is it too crowded? Too empty? Too cheap? Too expensive? Does it have our favourite dish? Why don't we try something new for a change?

'And . . .' he exchanged the spoon

momentarily for his Cross pen and brand new notebook, 'I think Truffert deserves a vote of thanks. The blending of all the ingredients has been done to perfection. No single one stands out; those that might have done—the chilli, the Calvados and lemon juice—have all been used with restraint and understanding.'

Nobody could accuse him of not doing his best to keep Amber's mind off the vexed question of Corby's non-appearance. Whether or not he was succeeding was another matter.

Even Pommes Frites was looking restive, as though he had heard it all before.

The lobster bisque disposed of, Monsieur Pamplemousse fortified himself by draining a glass of draught cider. All too aware of the fact that he was beginning to sound like a walking advertisement for Norman cuisine, he embarked on the subject of escalopes while they awaited their arrival. There was nothing else he could think of to talk about.

'It is another typical dish from the Auge Valley; the veal is cooked in a mixture of butter and groundnut oil, and the sauce made from double cream and mushrooms. The main difference in this case according to Truffert is that instead of adding Calvados, the chef uses a dry vermouth and it is served with creamed sorrel.'

'It sounds like another "must" for the private collection,' said Amber. 'What's with sorrel anyway?'

'Sorrel,' said Monsieur Pamplemousse, 'is one of the oldest culinary plants known to man. It is used all over Europe in cooking, as an aid to digesting the food, and for treating all manner of ailments, from bad breath to fixing loose teeth.'

'Are you trying to tell me something again?' said Amber.

Above the net curtaining across the lower part of the window Monsieur Pamplemousse caught sight of a group of heads peering in to see how service was progressing, so he hastily tried another tack.

'It is a sign of the times,' he mused. 'Ever since the No Smoking rule came in people spend more time outside restaurants having a quick puff between courses than they do inside it. Ask any street cleaner who has to clear up the butts—their workload has doubled.

'Anyway,' he continued, aware that Pommes Frites had suddenly come to life and was sitting up at the ready, nostrils quivering— probably indicating the imminent arrival of the next course, 'it makes a change from the "Shall we? Shan't we?" brigade.

'It takes all sorts. There was a monk sheltering from the rain just now, black habit and all. He took one look inside and he was off like a shot—'

The full import of what he had just said took a moment or two to penetrate.

'Did it have a hood?' demanded Amber.

243

'It did . . .'

'Jesus wept!'

Grabbing her evening bag, Amber leapt to her feet and was out through the door before he had a chance to say any more.

Ignoring the imminent arrival of the main course, Monsieur Pamplemousse, with Pommes Frites at his heels, followed suit, but she was already way ahead of them.

Weaving his way in and out of the parked cars in the central reservation, he was about to emerge on the side nearest the marina when he heard her call out.

Seconds later there came the unmistakable sound of a revolver. First one shot, then two in quick succession. Heart in his mouth, he came to an abrupt halt.

Signalling Pommes Frites to stay at his side, he began inching his way forward around the side of a van, then almost immediately froze as he found himself confronted by the barrel of a gun.

He recognised it at once: a semi-automatic Russian Baikal 9mm conversion. Capable of firing ten rounds, assuming it had a full magazine to begin with, that meant there were seven left.

Almost imperceptibly, he began moving his left hand slowly upwards.

The barrel of the gun moved too, but in a downward direction.

'Don't even think it,' said a voice.

Normally Monsieur Pamplemousse would have put the odds in favour of Pommes Frites, but he knew he would never forgive himself if the worst happened. It was a no-win situation.

He closed his eyes. 'I shall count up to ten,' he said. 'And then I never want to see you again.'

'Who's counting?' came a whisper.

Despite the warmth of the July rain, a shiver ran down his spine as he first of all felt the barrel of the gun against his stomach, then the speaker's lips against his. They were ice cold.

It was several moments before he was able to carry on, and by then he had lost count of where he had got to anyway.

When he eventually opened his eyes Amber was nowhere to be seen.

Pommes Frites was clearly all for going after her, but at a sign from his master he relaxed. Crossing over to the marina, he peered into it and, having drawn a blank, looked over his shoulder to await further instructions.

It was a strange turn of events. One moment Monsieur Pamplemousse and the girl had been happily talking about food, or so it seemed, although in his view it had been rather one-sided, the next moment they were having some kind of disagreement. That hadn't lasted more than a moment or two before it was a case of kiss and make up. Or was it? The girl had certainly disappeared; leaving his master mopping his brow with the present she had given him.

It was all very puzzling.

CHAPTER ELEVEN

'A woman in the Mafia!' exclaimed Monsieur Leclercq. 'Whatever is the world coming to, Aristide?'

'They have been driving trains on the Metro for some years now,' said Monsieur Pamplemousse. 'And buses.'

'Have they really? *Extraordinaire!*' The Director sounded relieved that he normally drove himself into the office.

For all his worldly experience, he led a sheltered life by most people's standards. Like many of those occupying positions of power, he had lost touch with what it was like to be a member of the rank and file. Worse still, he had no idea that he had.

'Other women have even been sent into space,' said Monsieur Pamplemousse.

'So the news isn't all bad,' said Monsieur Leclercq.

Catching sight of the expression on Monsieur Pamplemousse's face, he discarded an object he had been playing with and lay back in his bed.

'Forgive my somewhat jaundiced responses, Aristide, but I am not a good patient, I fear, and much as I respect members of the opposite sex—indeed, one sometimes wonders where we would be without them—they are inclined to fuss and ask awkward questions. I love Chantal dearly, but I do miss going into the office. If only they could all be like Véronique and come and go as required at the press of a buzzer.

'Anyway, enough of my complaining . . . you had reached the point where Corby, having dyed his bathrobe black, encountered unforeseen difficulties drying it . . .'

'Something any woman would have foreseen,' said Monsieur Pamplemousse. 'It was made of extremely thick material.'

'Yes, yes,' said the Director wearily, 'but if she was remotely like my wife he would never have heard the last of it. In any case, what was he doing wearing it while out and about in Caen late at night? It was asking for trouble.'

'I think his purpose was two-fold,' said Monsieur Pamplemousse. 'Most of all he needed to have it thoroughly dry before he moved on, but he also probably thought it was a good opportunity to test its effectiveness as a disguise under field conditions.

'Unfortunately it began to rain, undoing all his good work. And even more unfortunately for him, he happened to seek shelter in the very restaurant where we were dining—'

247

'A thousand to one chance,' hazarded Monsieur Leclercq.

'Not really. The area around the marina was an obvious place to take a stroll. It was away from the bright lights, and the restaurant was one of the few along the Quai Vendeuvre with a canopy outside affording some kind of shelter. People were constantly looking in to see what was going on. I imagine he could hardly believe his eyes when he saw us sitting there.'

'And the girl—the one you call Amber—shot him. Just like that. In cold blood?

'Only after a chase in the pouring rain,' said Monsieur Pamplemousse.

'Hardly mitigating circumstances in a court of law, Aristide!'

'That aspect is not something which normally causes members of the Mafia to lose any sleep,' said Monsieur Pamplemousse.

'And you have not seen or heard anything from her since?'

Monsieur Pamplemousse shook his head. To have told the whole truth might have prolonged the conversation far beyond his original intentions.

Monsieur Leclercq fell silent while he tried to picture the scene.

'I suppose,' he said at last, 'from all you have told me, the world is probably a better place without Corby. He was a blot on the escutcheon of our profession.'

'Almost certainly,' said Monsieur Pamplemousse. 'And it was as clean a way as any to go. Marinas don't recognise carbon footprints.'

'Nevertheless,' said Monsieur Leclercq, 'it must have come as a shock to you. Had you no inkling of the kind of person the girl was?'

Monsieur Pamplemousse opened his wallet and removed the photograph he had taken of Amber at the *gare*, and which he'd had printed during his shopping expedition in Caen.

The Director scanned it with interest. 'I do see the problem. It wouldn't have occurred to me, either. I doubt if you would have been her first beau, Pamplemousse. Nor her last. Unless, of course . . .'

Monsieur Pamplemousse hastily disabused him of the thought.

'You are a funny chap, Aristide,' said the Director unexpectedly. 'What stopped you?'

'When the possibility arose,' said Monsieur Pamplemousse, 'I had some telephone calls to make. I also felt Pommes Frites had his reservations, and I trust his judgement. He doesn't miss much. Little things . . . like when she adjusted my trouser leg ends on the very first morning . . .'

'Pretty forward stuff,' said Monsieur Leclercq. 'He had a point. That is strictly wives only territory.'

'You have experienced it, Monsieur?'

'It happened soon after Chantal and I met.

It was at a golf club and I was wearing plus fours at the time—an invention of *Les Anglais*. She had never come across anything quite like them before. We have laughed about it many times since.'

'I suspect Amber was actually rather lonely,' said Monsieur Pamplemousse. 'There is such a thing as being too beautiful. Men either think they must be spoken for, or they see them as a plaything. The first wasn't so, and the second was not what she wanted.

'It was hard at times to tell which part of her life was real and which was make-believe.'

'When did you begin to suspect her?'

'Quite early on. She seemed too good to be true. So much so, I began laying traps by planting some loaded questions. It is an old trick much used during the last war when interrogating suspect spies.

'First of all you lull them into a false sense of security, then you casually slip a glaringly false statement into the conversation.

'She told me that after leaving the Crazy Horse she worked for, among others, Pierre Gagnaire and Alain Ducasse, so I brought up the subject of Paul Bocuse's 80th birthday celebration, suggesting it took place at Versailles and that Ducasse did all the cooking.'

'And she fell for it?' exclaimed the Director. 'I would have thought it was common knowledge the venue was the ballroom of the

Hôtel de Paris in Monte Carlo. Chefs came from all over the world to help prepare the dishes. It was a magnificent affair. I remember it well. No wonder your suspicions were aroused, Aristide.'

'Not only that,' said Monsieur Pamplemousse, 'but she went on about it a shade too long.

'There were other minor matters: vagueness about Corby's background in general and how they first met. At the same time she certainly knew more about the restaurant business than she was prepared to let on. I felt I was preaching to the converted. She automatically formed a very neat Bishop's Hat with her napkin when we were leaving the restaurant in Bernay, and although she said that since going to America she had spent all her time in New York, she spoke as though she had first-hand experience of the problems restaurateurs face in Las Vegas.'

'You did very well, Pamplemousse,' said the Director approvingly. 'So we have no cause for alarm.'

'I think I can safely reassure you on that score, Monsieur.'

'Good. Good. Tell me, as a matter of interest, how did she bring the gun into the country? I thought they were very hot on such things these days.'

'She had no need to. She must have picked it up when she got here. I rang an old colleague and he brought me up to date.

'They are manufactured in the Russian town of Izhevsk, home to the AK47 and some eighty per cent of other Russian firearms. Originally designed as a lightweight protective weapon for firing tear gas, it is made of solid steel, so it lends itself to easy conversion for firing live ammunition. Converted in Lithuania, it has become known as the "hitman's gun". In France, they come shrink-wrapped in a box, and cost around €250. They are also small enough to fit into a lady's evening bag.'

The Director passed the photograph back to Monsieur Pamplemousse.

'I take it you will be handing this in to the appropriate quarter?'

Monsieur Pamplemousse shook his head.

The Director looked shocked. 'Pamplemousse! I am surprised at you. It makes a mockery of that old adage: "once a policeman, always a policeman".'

'With respect, Monsieur, I beg to differ. There are times when even a policeman has to act as both prosecuting counsel and counsel for the defence. And then, having weighed up all the evidence, take on the role of judge and jury into the bargain.'

'And what would be your verdict, Aristide?'

'Guilty, but with extenuating circumstances. One needs to be pragmatic about these things. I doubt if many people will lose much sleep over Corby's disappearance, and a whole host of others will breathe a sigh of relief.

'There were times in the old days when turning a blind eye was the order of the day. Nowadays that isn't quite so easy. For once, I shall indulge in the luxury of taking my time about it. That apart, there is *Le Guide*'s involvement to think of, the attendant publicity is the very thing you wished to avoid.'

Monsieur Leclercq sat up straight and extended a hand. 'Pamplemousse,' he said, 'there will always be a position for you in our legal department, but I sincerely hope you won't see fit to make the change.'

Patently, Monsieur Leclercq had other matters on his mind. Having got Corby off his chest, he could hardly wait to change the subject. Reaching out for the object he had been toying with, he held it up for Monsieur Pamplemousse to see.

'It is what is known as an iPhone,' he announced. 'An extraordinary device. It is hard to picture, I know, but I have it on good authority that this tiny piece of equipment is more sophisticated than a dozen office computers put together.

'Through the medium of the web, it can not only tell you where you are at any given moment, it can plan your route to wherever it is you are going, update you on road conditions, tell you what is on at the local cinema when you get there, and while you are waiting, you can listen to music, take pictures or play games. The list of all it has to offer is practically endless and it is growing all the time.

'The President of the United States of America presented its forerunner—what is known as an iPod, to Queen Elizabeth of England when they first met. It contained all her favourite tunes including "You'll Never Walk Alone" and "Diamonds are a Girl's Best Friend" . . .'

Clearly the Director had been got at since they last spoke.

'I am sure she will find it very useful . . .' began Monsieur Pamplemousse, 'but . . .'

There were times when Monsieur Leclercq almost took his breath away. On the one hand, when it came to advances in the world of photography, he prided himself on being at the cutting edge of the latest developments, forever updating *Le Guide*'s issue camera. In other areas, they completely by-passed him.

It was tempting to suggest that, had he possessed an iPhone when he was lying in the ditch, he could have used the time to good effect.

'No buts, Pamplemousse,' said the Director severely. 'Chantal gave me this one to help while away the time, and it has proved to be an eye-opener. It is no exaggeration to say that inside this tiny device is where our future lies.

'What is particularly germane to our function in life is that wherever you happen to be, at the press of a button it can not only give you a list of the nearest restaurants, but provide you with an up to date list of their menus as well.

'Times are changing, Aristide, and we must change with them. We need to school ourselves to adjust to the world as it is, not as we would like it to be. It is not too much to say that it will enable our own carbon footprint to do its bit towards the common goal. People will no longer need to carry *Le Guide* around with them as they do now . . . the world-wide easing of the weight load in itself will be considerable.

'But we must work fast. Michelin have already taken the first step in what I believe is known as "Going Global", and we must follow suit.

'It will need a person of taste and discernment to oversee it all . . . someone with the breadth of vision, the will power, and above all the willingness to embrace such a project with open arms so that we can move forward with speed to pastures new . . .'

Monsieur Pamplemousse felt his spirits rising. The Director was in his Napoleonic mode again; albeit a Napoleon lying prone in his bed, but nevertheless in fighting spirit and with his eye on the goal. It was inspirational to say the least, and he took a deep breath.

'I hardly know what to say, Monsieur. It will be a huge undertaking. I don't know what my wife will feel about it—'

'Ah, Doucette!' boomed the Director. 'She is a good lady. Always thinking of others. But tell her not to lose too much sleep. I shall manage to cope.'

'But, Monsieur—'

Monsieur Leclercq raised his hands. 'I know what you are about to say, Aristide. How will I manage to fit it in along with all my other responsibilities? Where there is a will, there is a way. It is an old saying, but a very true one nonetheless.'

Deep down Monsieur Pamplemousse had to admit to a feeling of relief. It had much in common with the moment when he mistakenly thought the Director was offering him a post in New York. In truth, he was perfectly happy with his present status in life.

'I must confess I still prefer doing things the old way,' he said. 'It keeps you in touch with reality.

'Human beings are gradually becoming more and more isolated from each other. These days, even making a telephone call lacks warmth. You never know whether the voice reading out an endless list of numbers to press, none of which correspond with who you really wish to speak to, is real or not. One has to be careful about losing one's temper in case for once it happens to be a real person. Many a time and oft I have come near to throwing my mobile out of the window.

'Soon there will be no surprises left in the world. Driving around and coming across places quite by chance will become a thing of the past, particularly if finding a good restaurant means that one day people will have no use for a printed guide.'

'That is *Deux Chevaux* thinking, Aristide,' said Monsieur Leclercq.

'That is partly why I like it,' said Monsieur Pamplemousse.

'Rest assured, Pamplemousse, there will still be a need for people to search them out and make an informed judgement in the first place. Perhaps more than ever, and that is where you come in. You and your colleagues will always be an indispensable link in the chain. Which reminds me . . .

'I am told the village blacksmith has finished his side of things and has handed your car back to the garage. Unfortunately, they are having problems with an audio warning system I am having fitted. It keeps saying there is no passenger door—'

'That is probably because there is no inside to the lock,' said Monsieur Pamplemousse. 'It has been like that for a number of years. There is some string under the front seat.'

'Ah,' said Monsieur Leclercq. 'In that case it is ready for collection. However, your mention of the front seat reminds me of another matter . . .'

Monsieur Pamplemousse braced himself,

257

but he was saved in the nick of time by a knock on the door; almost as though someone had been awaiting their cue.

There was a moment's pause, then Madame Leclercq entered.

'You have done quite enough talking for one morning, Henri,' she said briskly, as she set about tidying the bedclothes. 'The doctor is due any moment and he will be very cross with you.'

Monsieur Leclercq didn't actually say 'Not tonight, Josephine' as he sank back onto his pillow, but the thought was clearly there.

'How did you find Henri?' asked Chantal, as they made their way down the stairs.

'I think he is on the mend,' said Monsieur Pamplemousse cautiously. 'Time is a great healer.'

Chantal looked relieved. 'He hasn't been his usual self since the day I dropped him off at the *gare* in Lisieux to pick up your car. I can't help feeling it is partly my fault. He should have stayed in bed.'

'On top of everything else, he is suffering from something called Ornithophobia.'

'Oh dear,' said Monsieur Pamplemousse. 'It sounds painful.'

'Fear of anything with wings,' said Chantal. 'They only discovered it because I came across a boxed set of Alfred Hitchcock DVDs I had given him for his birthday. I thought it might cheer him up while he was in bed.

258

'Unfortunately, he chose to watch one called *The Birds* and it left him a shivering wreck. I really don't understand it.'

'A lot of people are nervous of them,' said Monsieur Pamplemousse. 'Especially when they get very close.'

'To make matters worse, he keeps sending people messages. He calls it "twittering". I suppose it must be some kind of side effect.'

'I shouldn't worry too much,' said Monsieur Pamplemousse. 'It is a new means of communication where you have to say things in less than 140 words. I doubt if he will keep it up for long.'

Chantal looked relieved. 'I have been saving these for you.' She pointed to a pile of journals on the hall table. 'They are all Pommes Frites' reviews.'

Monsieur Pamplemousse scanned the headline on the top copy: 'A STAR IS BORN!' he exclaimed.

'Henri has received some very nice ones, of course, but Pommes Frites even had one in an English journal. The headline was POETRY IN MOTIONS. I'm not quite sure what that one meant.'

'It sounds like an English play on words,' said Monsieur Pamplemousse, gathering up the pile. 'They love double meanings.'

When Chantal dropped him off at the garage to pick up his car she presented him with a parcel to take back to Paris.

'Henri says you must take great care of it on the way; no squeezing, and make sure you keep it upright. There is also something in there for Pommes Frites. It sounds like a Christmas present.'

'I suppose in a way it is,' said Monsieur Pamplemousse. 'We shall certainly treat it as such.'

*   *   *

'I must say, Aristide, it is a big bonus having you home much sooner than I expected,' said Doucette. 'When you phoned to say you were on your way to Alsace-Lorraine I thought you might be gone for weeks.'

'It feels much longer than it really was,' admitted Monsieur Pamplemousse. 'In the end we didn't get any further than Caen.'

'You must have been there when that priest was shot,' said Doucette. 'Very sad really. You probably know more about it than I do, but I gather he was found floating in a marina. At first the police assumed it was suicide, but it seems there were three bullet holes. One where they say it hurts most, and two in the temple, so they now think it could be murder.'

'I would have come to the same conclusion,' admitted Monsieur Pamplemousse dryly.

'Mind you,' said Doucette, 'he did sound a bit suspect. His behaviour once he came down from the pulpit was a matter of some concern. Reading between the lines, it sounds as though they have had their eyes on him for some while. What was he doing prowling around the marina at that time of night anyway, I would like to know? *And* in the pouring rain.'

Monsieur Pamplemousse stared at her. 'You don't mean . . .' he began 'You can't mean . . . it was a real one?'

'It could hardly have been a toy pistol,' said Doucette.

'I don't mean the gun,' said Monsieur Pamplemousse. 'I mean the priest.'

'Well, he didn't take the service on the Sunday, if that's anything to go by,' said Doucette. 'And no one has seen him since. *Paris Match* is implying choirboys can look forward to a more restful time in future, but you know what they are like.'

'*Sacre bleu!*' said Monsieur Pamplemousse.

'Aristide!' said Doucette. 'He was a priest, after all.'

For a moment or two he hardly heard what she was saying. His mind was in overdrive.

Such things weren't unknown, of course. They happened in the best-regulated circles. Sometimes they ended up gathering dust as an entry in the police files. At other times, if the press took it into their heads to make a meal of it, or politics were involved, it was another matter.

The English police were still licking their

wounds following the shooting of a suspected terrorist on the London Underground, and probably would be for years to come.

It was the 'being in a certain place at a certain time' syndrome yet again; although in this instance those involved must be feeling there was a lot to be said for it being a case of 'the wrong man in the wrong place at the wrong time'. Others might call it 'rough justice'.

What was it the American writer Saul Bellow had said when asked about the difference between ignorance and indifference? 'I don't know and I don't care!'

It would have been a salutary warning to Corby. He would feel the net was definitely closing in on him. As for Amber, wherever she was by now, she might never know the truth until such time as Corby showed his head again—if he ever did.

Reaching into his pocket, he produced a card that had been left for him at the hotel in Caen, read a pencilled number on the back, and reached for the phone.

'What now, Aristide?' asked Doucette. 'You've only just got back.'

'I want to find out what time *Boucherie Lamartine* opens in the morning, Couscous. Pommes Frites has an appointment with them, courtesy of Monsieur Leclercq. It might be as well to arrive there before it gets too crowded. It could be a long job.'

'Otherwise, there is no great hurry. I have a bottle of wine which needs to rest for a few days.'

The call completed, he turned the card over. It bore the name of a restaurant in Las Vegas, most of which had been obliterated by a message written in black.

'Any chance of coming to the Grand Reopening? I'm thinking of calling it "The Enigma". You could have the "day's special"— Sonofabitch Stew.'

He was about to tear the card into small pieces when he hesitated. He had yet to make a printout of the first picture he had taken of Amber and Pommes Frites. He had promised to send her a copy and a promise was a promise.

'Before you do anything else, Aristide,' said Doucette, 'your suit looks as though a visit to the cleaners wouldn't come amiss. I'll take it tomorrow.'

The words were hardly out of her mouth before he felt something tugging at his right trouser leg.

'I think Pommes Frites wants to go out,' said Doucette. 'It's been a long drive.'

'But he has only just—'

Monsieur Pamplemousse broke off as he glanced down and saw Pommes Frites looking up at him anxiously. He placed an index finger against his nose, indicating message received and understood. Pockets must first be emptied of all souvenirs.

'Good boy,' he said, when they were outside the apartment. 'What would I do without you?'

Pommes Frites wagged his tail. It was good to get something right at long last. But then, life with his master was full of surprises. No two days were ever the same and quite frankly, he wouldn't have had it any other way.

Monsieur Pamplemousse, on the other hand, was in a bit of a quandary. The news that the wrong person had got his comeuppance took a bit of getting used to. It also raised the question, should he, or should he not, accept the Director's gifts for a job that was, after all, only half done?

Pommes Frites would be looking forward to his visit to the butchers, there could be no going back on that.

The wine was another matter. Margaux 45 was renowned for its lasting qualities. Another week or so would hardly matter one way or the other.

The door to his apartment suddenly opened.

'Is there anything the matter, Aristide?' asked Doucette.

'I was thinking, Couscous,' said Monsieur Pamplemousse. 'Perhaps we could invite the Leclercqs over here for dinner one evening.'

'Do you think they would come?' asked Doucette.

'I'm sure they will if I say we want to share

the bottle of wine the Director gave me. I shall feel much better about it.'

'What shall I wear?' said Doucette, clearly thrown by the whole idea.

Monsieur Pamplemousse raised his eyes heavenwards as he pressed the lift button. Problems! Problems!

Who was it that said, 'You can't please all the people all the time?' At the end of the day, life mostly had to do with striking a happy balance.